"Doesn't anyone in this town believe in love?"

"Obviously some couples do," Hunter replied. "That's why they get married so often."

Bliss looked at his handsome, jaded face with a feeling of hopelessness. Although she knew the answer already, she asked, "You don't believe in love that lasts?"

"I believe people *think* it will last."

"When I fall in love, it will be forever."

"I hope it happens that way for you," he said with surprising gentleness. "But talk to me after you've been here a while—and you've fallen in and out of love a few times."

"I hope never to become as disillusioned as you are," she answered quietly.

He covered her hand tightly. "Believe it or not, we share the same values."

Was it possible they shared the same feelings, as well? She managed a smile. "Then there's hope for both of us. Maybe we'll find true love and live happily ever after."

Dear Reader,

Welcome to the Silhouette **Special Edition** experience! With your search for consistently satisfying reading in mind, every month the authors and editors of Silhouette **Special Edition** aim to offer you a stimulating blend of deep emotions and high romance.

The name Silhouette **Special Edition** and the distinctive arch on the cover represent a commitment—a commitment to bring you six sensitive, substantial novels each month. In the pages of a Silhouette **Special Edition**, compelling true-to-life characters face riveting emotional issues—and come out winners. Both celebrated authors and newcomers to the series strive for depth and dimension, vividness and warmth, in writing these stories of living and loving in today's world.

The result, we hope, is romance you can believe in. Deeply emotional, richly romantic, infinitely rewarding—that's the Silhouette **Special Edition** experience. Come share it with us—six times a month!

From all the authors and editors of Silhouette **Special Edition**,

Best wishes,

Leslie Kazanjian
Senior Editor

TRACY SINCLAIR
Miss Robinson Crusoe

Silhouette Special Edition

Published by Silhouette Books New York

America's Publisher of Contemporary Romance

Author of more than twenty-five Silhouette novels, **TRACY SINCLAIR** also contributes to various magazines and newspapers. She says her years as a photojournalist provided the most exciting adventures—and misadventures—of her life. An extensive traveler—from Alaska to South America, and most places in between—and a dedicated volunteer worker—from suicide-prevention programs to English-as-a-second-language instructor—the California resident has accumulated countless fascinating experiences, settings and acquaintances to draw on in plotting her romances.

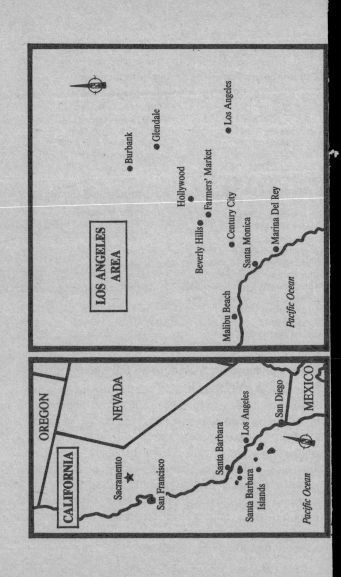

Chapter One

The two men in the elegantly furnished office were deep in conversation when the intercom buzzed.

"You asked me to remind you when it was five o'clock, Mr. Dennison," a woman's voice announced.

"Oh, right. Thanks, Carole."

The plush office was state of the art, befitting the head of entertainment for WBC, the top-rated television network. Dennison pushed a button on his console, activating a panel on the wall at the far end of the room. A section of the paneling slid aside, revealing a large TV screen. Another button was pressed to turn on the set. A team of news anchors were giving a lead-in to the upcoming story.

"This is an exciting moment," the female member of the team was saying. "The whole country is waiting for a glimpse of Bliss Goodwin, the courageous woman who managed to survive all alone on a deserted island for almost a year."

"It's a remarkable story," the male newscaster agreed. "She's already been dubbed Miss Robinson Crusoe by the press."

The camera cut away to a landing field where a large group of people were waiting on the tarmac as the door of a Navy jet swung open. A man in civilian clothes emerged from the plane.

"That must be the government representative, Steve. He was flown to the ship to escort Miss Goodwin home."

"And what a homecoming it is, Elaine. Hordes of reporters, politicians and movie stars are waiting to greet her. Los Angeles is rolling out the welcome mat."

"There she is!" the female anchor said excitedly.

The camera panned in for a close shot of the young woman who was standing on the steps, gazing at the crowd with a look of bewilderment.

"This is even better than I hoped for." Clay Dennison was staring at the screen with narrowed eyes that glittered with excitement. "Look at that face!"

Dan Kronsky was looking, but he obviously didn't share his boss's enthusiasm. "She's kind of plain-looking, except for the blond hair. And she's scrawny."

"Of course she's scrawny! What else would you expect after a year of living on nuts and berries, or whatever she ate. But look at that exquisite bone structure. Did you ever see such fantastic cheekbones? And check out those big blue eyes."

"You're full of surprises, chief," Dan said. "I thought you liked your women sexier."

"Don't be a jerk. This girl is a gold mine. A docudrama on her experience is going to send our ratings through the roof. Find out where she's staying, and send Sid around to buy the rights before the sharks start to gather."

"How high do you want him to go?"

"As high as necessary, but we should be able to get her for peanuts. What does a missionary know about money?"

"Can you imagine spending your whole life in the jungle teaching a bunch of natives not to run around buck-naked?"

"*I* can't, but that's what makes the story so great. It's got everything—action, danger, religion, sex." Rare animation lit the network chief's jaded face.

"Sex? I thought she was alone on that island."

"Meaning she didn't have to wear clothes, right? I think we'll get Mona Jensen to play the part. She's game for as much nudity as we can get away with, and she has the body for it. Get on this thing right away, Dan."

Bliss was already being beset by the sharks Dennison predicted would gather. The crowd of reporters and photographers closed in on her like those deadly fish scenting blood.

"How does it feel to be back in civilization?" a reporter shouted.

"What are your plans for the future? Are you going back to Africa?"

"What did you miss most on the island?" The question drew laughter from the crowd.

"Look over here, Bliss," a photographer called.

She automatically did as she was told, but the questions were being fired too rapidly to answer.

Finally, someone stuck a microphone in her face and said, "Give us a statement."

The sudden silence made her as nervous as all the shouted questions. In a soft, halting voice she said, "I'm very grateful to the men who rescued me, and all the people who have been helpful in so many ways."

The interrogation continued. "Do you have relatives in L.A.? Where are you going to stay?"

"Is it true that your whole family were missionaries?"

The official who had been on the plane with her said, "That's enough questions for now, ladies and gentlemen. Miss Goodwin is tired from the long flight." He took her arm and led her through the protesting throng to a waiting limousine.

Hunter Lord turned on the television set when he wandered into his den at five o'clock to make himself a drink. The two actions were force of habit. He didn't want to watch TV, and he didn't want a drink. Boredom was making him react like Pavlov's dog, he reflected disgustedly.

A long bar stretched along one wall of the luxurious room. While he got ice cubes out of the refrigerator under the counter, he glanced indifferently at the television screen. A cynical expression accentuated the ruggedness of his features as he watched the reporters besieging the slender, defenseless woman.

"A whole army of missionaries couldn't make a dent in this town," he muttered. "If you're smart, you'll go back where you came from."

A short, stocky man in a white coat and black trousers entered the den and gave him a disapproving look. "You might at least have put on shoes. I just waxed the floor."

A grin displayed white teeth in Hunter's deeply tanned face. "A man's home is his castle, Max."

"That doesn't mean the king has to walk around in his bare feet. And don't sit down if your suit is wet," the manservant warned, appraising the bathing trucks that were all his employer wore.

"Lighten up. If I wanted someone to nag me, I'd get married."

"You can't afford a wife," Max answered calmly.

"I can't afford you, either." Discontent returned to darken Hunter's face. "Why don't you find a job with someone who can pay your salary on time?"

"Who would hire me? After working for you for ten years, everybody figures I must be crazy."

Hunter smiled unwillingly. "You're not the easiest person in the world to live with, either."

"At least I don't sit around the pool all day sulking and getting flabby."

The accusation was unwarranted on at least one count. Hunter's lean frame was composed mostly of bone and muscle. Broad shoulders tapered to narrow hips and long, well-formed legs. The easy coordination of his movements was the mark of an athlete in top shape.

"I wasn't sulking," he said. "I was contemplating my navel. Far Eastern religions say that promotes tranquility."

"But it doesn't pay the mortgage. Why don't you stop being so pigheaded?" Max demanded. "You've given new meaning to the term 'independent producer.'"

Hunter scowled ferociously as he splashed Scotch into his glass. "The studios owe me one. I've made millions for them with movies pitched to the IQ of morons. Is it

too much to ask for a chance to make *one* socially re-
deeming film? *Winter's End* is a script I believe in.''

"Maybe so, but until some studio agrees with you and
puts up the money, why don't you go back to work?
Clay Dennison keeps dangling offers in front of your
nose.''

"Because my name on a production means something. But I'm through being exploited.'' Without waiting for Max's rebuttal, he stalked back to the pool.

Bliss was bewildered by her celebrity status and the
alien world she was thrust into. After living a good part
of her life in an African village, Los Angeles seemed bi-
zarre. The traffic, the crowds, the noise were all confusing.

Her relief at being rescued had turned to panic on the
ship when she realized she was all alone in the world,
with no money and nowhere to go. Then, unaccount-
ably, benefits started to rain down on her.

The limousine that whisked her from the airport was
sent by the hotel that provided her with a luxurious suite
free of charge. She was told to sign for meals and anything else she wanted. Enough clothes for a dozen
women were delivered, also gratis.

"You must have the wrong room,'' she told the bellman who delivered the first batch. "I didn't order these
things.''

"They have your name on them.''

"It has to be a mistake,'' she insisted. "I can't afford
to buy anything.''

"I wouldn't worry about that,'' he said. "The stores
will get their money's worth from the publicity. You're
big news, Miss Goodwin.''

His assurance proved correct. When Bliss phoned the stores that had sent the clothes, she was told they were indeed complimentary.

The same was true with the hairdresser and manicurist who came to her suite the morning after she arrived. Bliss again tried to explain, with considerable embarrassment, that she couldn't afford their services. But they waved her explanation aside.

"The shop is taking care of it. Besides, it's a privilege to work on you, Miss Goodwin," Martha, the hairdresser, replied. "You're a real heroine."

"Scarcely that. I didn't plan on getting caught in a monsoon."

"It's a wonder you weren't drowned," the manicurist marveled. Her name was Anna.

"It's even more of a miracle that she was rescued from that little bitty dot in the ocean," Martha said. "You're lucky the Navy was looking for a site to conduct their tests."

Bliss gave a small rueful laugh. "Fortunately they came ashore to be sure it was uninhabited. It would have been ironic if I'd been blown up after surviving a shipwreck."

Martha shuddered. "I never did like boats. You wouldn't catch *me* out in the ocean all alone."

"I wasn't—" Bliss stopped abruptly. "I'd rather not talk about it if you don't mind."

The two women exchanged understanding glances. To ease the awkward moment, Martha felt the texture of the long blond hair that cascaded down Bliss's back.

"A conditioner is definitely in order after I cut your hair," she decided. "You don't want to leave it this length, do you?"

"No, it's a terrible bother. I would have hacked it off myself except that it was more convenient to wear it in a braid on the island," Bliss answered.

"It's a shame in a way. You have gorgeous hair." Martha let the bright strands slip through her fingers. "I'll leave it shoulder length."

"Whatever you like," Bliss replied indifferently.

Anna, the manicurist, was clucking over Bliss's nails. "There's not much here to work with. I'll have to sculpture them."

"What's that?" Bliss couldn't have cared less what either woman did, but her curiosity was aroused.

"It's a way of lengthening nails with liquid plastic. I can make them as long as you like."

"I don't want false fingernails," Bliss protested.

"They aren't exactly false; they're built onto your real ones. You won't be able to tell them from your own," Anna said reassuringly.

Without giving her time for further objections they started to work. The equipment they'd brought transformed the suite into a portable beauty shop that was almost as busy as the one downstairs. They were interrupted constantly by the phone and the doorbell.

Flowers and packages arrived in a steady stream, along with a quantity of mail. The phone calls were mainly from newspapers, magazines and the representatives of television shows and movie companies.

"You won't have to worry about money, Miss Goodwin," Martha said after returning from taking yet another message. "That one was from *National Spectator*. They want to pay you for your story. He said to tell you the sky's the limit if you'll give them an exclusive."

"She doesn't want to do business with that scandal sheet," Anna said disapprovingly.

"Is that what it is?" Bliss asked.

Anna gave a ladylike sniff. "You might as well pose for *Casanova Magazine*."

"There was a message from them waiting for me when I got here yesterday," Bliss said. "Is something wrong with them, too?"

"Not if you don't mind being photographed in the nude."

"I'd be careful what I signed if I were you," Martha warned. "You're a hot property right now, and everybody's out to make a buck off you."

Bliss frowned. "You mean none of the offers I've received are legitimate?"

"They all are, but some of them want more for their money than others."

"I'll admit I was surprised at the fuss people were making," Bliss said slowly.

"What you need is an agent, so people don't take advantage of you," Anna advised.

Martha agreed. "You've been out of touch for a long time."

That was certainly true. Bliss felt like a dinosaur. So many things were foreign to her here, even something as commonplace as a remote-control device. The bellman had to tell her what it was for. She was familiar with television, of course. Contrary to what people thought, she hadn't spent her entire life in the jungle prior to the boating tragedy. But the ever-present examples of modern technology that everyone else took for granted astonished her.

The subject of her celebrity and what to do about it was dropped when Martha turned off the hair dryer and stepped back to view the results of her labor. "How do you like it?" she asked, handing Bliss a mirror.

A stranger stared back at her. The long hair she'd braided and tied with a palm frond now just grazed her shoulders. The gleaming mass formed a pale frame around her face, accentuating the tan she'd acquired on the island.

"You look fantastic!" Anna exclaimed.

"Even without makeup," Martha concurred. "But you don't need much," she advised Bliss. "Just some blue eye shadow to accentuate the color of your eyes, and maybe a touch of peach-colored lipstick. I can do your face for you while I'm here if you like."

These women obviously had no conception of the conditions she'd lived under. "I don't have any makeup," Bliss said.

"Of course! How could you?" Belated realization hit both women. "I'll go downstairs and get everything you need."

"That really isn't necessary. I didn't mention it for that reason."

Her protests fell on deaf ears. Martha went down to the beauty salon and returned with a lavish array of cosmetics, most of which Bliss had never used.

When she confessed as much, the other woman insisted on doing a complete makeup job on her. The effect was startling. The new hairdo had been a surprise, but Martha's latest handiwork came as a shock.

The face she created had a luminous glow enhanced by the slight tint of color over the cheekbones, as though they'd been warmed by the sun that had given Bliss's skin its golden hue. The skillfully applied mascara darkened the blond tips of her eyelashes, accentuating their length and thickness, and the peach lipstick gave definition to her softly curved mouth.

"You're a genius, Martha," Anna declared when the job was done.

"Look what I had to work with. Well, what do you think?" she asked Bliss.

"I'll need a little time to get used to it," Bliss answered hesitantly.

"I can imagine." Martha glanced at her watch. "And speaking of time, I'd better get back. My next appointment is due in ten minutes."

After the women left, Bliss wandered aimlessly through the suite, feeling vaguely disturbed by the change in herself. She didn't even *look* the same anymore.

Loneliness settled over her like a cloak, even though the phone was ringing at the moment. The calls weren't from friends—she didn't have any here. Before melancholy could overwhelm her she left the suite, hoping a walk would chase away the blues.

A magazine stand in the lobby caught her eye, and she went over to look for a copy of *Casanova Magazine*. The girl on the cover was tasteless enough, but the photographs inside made Bliss's mouth drop open. This was the kind of thing they wanted to pay her to do? Her expression was grim as she replaced the magazine and searched fruitlessly for a copy of *National Spectator*. The hotel didn't carry tabloid newspapers.

A much larger stand several blocks away was well stocked with them, including the one she wanted. Bliss's lip curled with disgust as she read the headings of the stories on the front page:

Woman Claims Alien from
Outer Space Raped Her.

Whose Body Lies in Daniel Gibb's Grave?
Parents Say Not Their Son's.

Star's Wife Tells All about Orgies
in Their Mansion

These people were freaks! Is that what the publishers considered *her*? Martha's warning was certainly timely. Bliss shuddered to think what would have happened if she'd accepted the offer of either publication.

At least these two were easy to check out, but what about the other offers she'd received? With no one to advise her, she'd have to refuse all of them, even though money was a pressing problem. Bliss was even more dispirited as she retraced her steps to the hotel.

"What do you mean she won't sign?" Clay Dennison's manicured fingers tightened around the receiver. "Did you let someone beat you out?" After listening for a moment he said, "Don't hand me that! Everything's for sale if you offer enough." Cutting the caller's answer short he said, "No, I don't want you to keep trying. I'll get someone who can do the job."

Slamming down the phone, he looked disgustedly at the man on the other side of the desk. "Sid blew it. The missionary won't sign."

It took a moment for Dan to make the connection, then he asked, "Who got there first?"

"Nobody, according to Sid. He says she told him she's not accepting any offers for her story."

"Well, it isn't the end of the world. We can make a docudrama without her okay. That's what all the other networks will be doing."

"Exactly. So why should the viewers watch ours?"

"We'll have bigger stars and maybe a name producer," Dan suggested.

The sullen look on Clay's face changed to speculation. "You may have something there. We'll offer a quality production instead of the schlock our competition will turn out."

"Sure. We don't need the girl."

"That's where you're wrong. Her stamp of approval will give us the edge. People want to believe what they're watching is the inside story."

"But if she won't sign?" Dan asked.

"When one kind of bait doesn't work, you try another. The newspapers say everyone is sending her gifts. What do you suppose a woman who's been out of circulation for a year would like to have delivered to her door?"

Dan's chuckle had a ribald sound. "How about Rick Boland or Trent Cramer? They're the hottest things on the tube this year."

Clay shook his head. "She's probably never heard of them. Besides, I propose killing two birds with one stone. I'm going to send the hunter after Little Red Riding Hood."

"You don't mean—"

"Hunter Lord," Clay said with satisfaction. "He's not only the big-name producer we need, he's also dynamite with women. They go nuts over that brooding Heathcliff act of his. If he tells the girl to sign, I guarantee you she'll sign."

"You've flipped, chief. He wouldn't touch a deal like this with a broom handle."

"He will if I finance that script he's been bugging me about. How big a turkey is it?"

"Actually, it's a damn fine property," Dan replied. "That's the trouble—it's too good for TV. The audience for quality stuff is limited."

"We'll make it on a shoestring." Clay punched out a number on the phone. "Who knows? Even if nobody but the critics watch the thing, we might get an Emmy nomination out of it. That would be worth—" He leaned back in his chair with the look of a cat about to lap cream. "Hunter, baby, where have you been keeping yourself? I don't like to lose track of old friends."

Bliss was up early the next morning from force of habit. After showering and dressing in tailored white pants and a pale blue silk shirt, she had nothing to do. To pass the time she tried her hand at recreating the face Martha had given her the day before, then wondered why she'd bothered. Nobody would see it, and she wasn't that crazy about her altered self.

She wandered out onto the terrace to stare broodingly at the vast sprawling city. Was there a place in it for her? She'd have to try to find one soon. A feeling of panic rose in her throat at the thought of leaving this sanctuary, however impersonal it was. She had no idea where to begin.

The ringing of the doorbell made her sigh. More packages probably, things she neither needed nor wanted. Or perhaps the bellman was bringing her daily assortment of weird requests. She couldn't believe the number of proposals she'd received from men who said they'd fallen in love with her.

The man at the door wasn't a bellman, however. He was imposingly tall, with an athlete's body and rugged features. The saturnine expression on his face made her uneasy. It changed almost immediately to a smile of great charm.

"Miss Goodwin? I'm Hunter Lord. May I come in?"

"Well, I..." Her hesitation was ineffectual. He brushed by her into the living room.

"I'd like to talk to you about a business matter." He indicated a chair. "Please sit down."

Bliss did as she was told, although it occurred to her that he was acting as though he were the host and she the guest.

His eyes lit with male appreciation as he took a better look at her. "You aren't exactly what I expected."

"In what way?"

"You looked different on television—the day you arrived."

Bliss gave him a faint smile. "I suppose so. I was wearing clothes donated by some sailors on the Navy ship." She'd had to belt the oversize garments tightly and roll up the sleeves and cuffs.

"It's more than that." His eyes roamed over her face.

"I had my hair cut."

"Perhaps that's it," he agreed absently, continuing to gaze at her.

Bliss felt uncomfortably like a butterfly about to be added to a collection. "What was it you wanted to talk about?"

His bemused expression changed as though a curtain had dropped behind his eyes. "I represent the World Broadcasting Company, Miss Goodwin."

Before he could continue, Bliss said firmly, "You're wasting your time, Mr. Lord. I've already been contacted by a man from your company. I'll give you the same answer I gave him—I'm not interested."

"If it's a question of money..."

"You all seem to think *money* is a magic word," she exclaimed in annoyance.

His smile was a mere twitch of facial muscles. "It's been known to open more doors than a key."

"Maybe with some people, not with me."

"What do you have against money, Miss Goodwin?"

"I can do without it," she snapped, thinking of how she'd have to earn it.

"I see." His gaze traveled over her expensively simple outfit and perfectly coiffed hair. "When the newspapers said you were a missionary, I just naturally assumed you weren't...uh...overly affluent."

"That was a safe assumption," she replied ironically.

"Yet you've refused all offers for your story."

"Nobody's interested in my story. All any of you want to do is exploit me! I've had offers from a disgusting magazine to pose in the nude, from people who want me to endorse products I've never heard of, from a yellow journal that would trivialize my whole life. What do you want, Mr. Lord? To put me in a sideshow? Come see Bliss Goodwin, queen of the jungle?"

He sat quietly through her tirade, a look of understanding on his strong face. "I sympathize with you, Miss Goodwin. I know something about exploitation myself."

She doubted that. This man looked as though he could take care of himself. Intelligence shone out of his steady eyes. He would be more apt to be the one doing the manipulating, but Bliss didn't intend to be a victim.

"Then you understand why I don't want my name associated with any of you," she said more calmly.

"Unfortunately you don't have a choice. Oh sure, you can refuse to endorse inferior products or to appear in sleazy magazines, but you can't stop anyone from writing about you or making a movie of your experience. That's news, and the people's right to know is protected by law."

"How about my right to privacy?" she asked, outraged.

His smile revealed even white teeth. "You gave up that right when you used your courage to survive on that island."

"I almost wish they'd left me there," she muttered.

"Come on, things aren't so bad." He glanced around the luxurious suite. "You'll have to admit this is a step up from a grass shack."

"At least that belonged to me." Bliss twisted her slim fingers together unconsciously as the familiar fluttering in her stomach commenced. "The management hasn't said anything to me yet, but I can't stay here indefinitely."

"You don't plan to go back to Africa?"

"There isn't anything there for me anymore," she answered simply.

"Your work?" he asked.

She sighed. "More media misinformation. I was never a missionary, my parents were. They took me to Africa when I was ten years old. I did grow up in a native village, but when I was old enough they sent me to a college in Nairobi. I wanted to come back to America to go to school, but it cost too much."

Hunter's brow furrowed. "Forgive me, but . . . you were able to get into college without a high school diploma?"

"By passing the entrance exams. Mother taught me and the other children. She had been a college professor in this country." Bliss gave him a lopsided smile. "Sorry if I'm spoiling my image."

"On the contrary, this is fascinating." He did look intrigued. "But after college you must have gone back to join your parents."

"I didn't plan to. I wanted to return to the States and teach—education was my major. But my mother wasn't well, and Dad asked me to come back and help out until she got better. So I went. It wasn't long after that that the . . . the accident occurred." Her eyes darkened with remembered pain.

"You said there wasn't anything to go back for now," he said slowly.

"My parents were in the boat with me. Dad knew the weather was chancy, but we had to visit another village. The road through the jungle would have taken twice as long and been hard on Mother, so he decided to risk it." Bliss stared down at her locked fingers. "They didn't make it to the island."

"I'm so sorry." Hunter's voice throbbed with sincerity.

"I don't know why I'm telling you all this," she murmured.

She looked so vulnerable that he clasped her hands impulsively. "It's good to let things out. You can't keep all that grief bottled up inside."

His sympathy was almost her undoing. He was so big and solid that for one fleeting moment she wanted to throw herself into his arms and shift her burdens to his broad shoulders.

Instead, she carefully withdrew her hands. "I'm not acting much like a private person, am I?"

"Everyone needs a friend, Bliss," he answered quietly. "I'd like to be yours if you'll let me."

"Even if I don't sign your contract?" Her blue eyes were very direct.

He met them squarely with his hazel ones. "That wasn't a condition of my offer."

His straightforwardness was convincing. "I do need to talk to someone."

"Tell me what's troubling you," he said gently.

"I have a big problem. I need a job and a place to live, and I don't know where to look for either one."

"What kind of work can you do?"

"I graduated with a degree in education, but I never taught in a regular school. When I called the L.A. School District, they said I needed teaching credentials before they could hire me. My degree from Nairobi didn't impress them."

"Surely you could take some sort of equivalency test."

"Perhaps, but everything would take time, and I have to go to work right away." She bit her lip to stop it from quivering. "I don't have a penny to my name. What will I do if the hotel puts me out?"

"It won't come to that," he soothed.

"I don't want to be a charity case," she protested. "It was wonderful of them to give me this lovely suite, but I can't freeload indefinitely."

"They're getting their money's worth. The whole world has heard of The Beverly Gardens by now. But that doesn't solve your problem." He hesitated. "Don't get the wrong idea, but why not accept our offer? The money would tide you over until you got settled and found work."

She stiffened. "I might have known!"

"I'm not trying to pressure you, Bliss," he said patiently. "I'm only offering good advice. The network will do your story whether you sign with them or not. You might as well get something out of it."

"If they really could do it without my approval, why should they pay me?"

"Because every other network will be doing the same thing, but your version would be the official one, which would guarantee the ratings. If you sign a contract, you'll get to tell it like it was. Otherwise, they'll fill in the blanks with a lot of sensationalism that might make you very unhappy."

"I could sue!" she said indignantly.

"Can you match the network's resources?" When she stared at him hopelessly he urged, "Take the money, Bliss. I promise I'll do everything in my power to make a tasteful film."

"What do you have to do with it?"

"I'd be the producer."

She looked at him curiously. "You're a rather important errand boy."

"Not really. Producers are a dime a dozen."

"I doubt that. Does your job depend on getting my signature?"

"No. I could produce a movie, anyway—if I wanted to."

"You don't want to do it without me?"

His hesitation was imperceptible. "Let's just say I'd rather make a film that contained some semblance of truth."

"I'd like that, too."

He looked at her thoughtfully. "How would you like to be a consultant? That would solve both your problems. You could keep us honest and have an income at the same time."

She examined the idea with dawning enthusiasm. "I could rent an apartment if I had a job."

"And buy a car," he suggested.

"Oh, I don't think so. The traffic here is horrendous."

"True, but a car is a necessity in Los Angeles. You do know how to drive, don't you?"

"I drove a Jeep in the bush, but the only obstacles to watch out for there were elephants and rhinos."

"Did you hit any?"

"No, it isn't a good idea."

Hunter chuckled. "You'll do just fine in L.A."

"I don't know how to thank you. I was feeling downright desperate before you came. You've thrown me a lifeline."

"I really think this is the best thing for you to do, Bliss. In spite of the fact that I stand to benefit, too. I wouldn't advise you to sign otherwise."

"I believe you."

A muscle twitched in his square jaw. "You'll have to learn not to be so trusting."

"I have to trust someone," she said simply. "I can't do it all alone anymore. If I've made a mistake about you, I'll have to live with it."

"I'll try not to let you down." He looked at her broodingly. "Just remember that life—modern life, anyway—is made up of compromises."

She smiled. "As long as you don't film my grass shack with drapes and an air-conditioning unit."

"It's hard to imagine anyone living like you did for so long."

She turned her head to gaze out the window, reliving the terror of tropical storms that threatened to sweep her into the angry sea, the loneliness of long nights with only the moon for light.

"I'm sorry." His voice was muted. "I didn't mean to remind you."

"It doesn't matter. I suppose the memory will always stay with me."

"No," he said forcefully. "The past is over. You're starting a whole new life."

"I wonder if I'll ever fit in here." Her face was wistful. "I don't want to be a curiosity the rest of my days."

"Anyone would be proud to be like you," he said in a husky voice. "You're a very special person."

Something electric leaped between them for a moment, a sexual awareness of each other. Bliss looked away awkwardly, feeling embarrassment at her involuntary reaction. Had he noticed? She certainly didn't want him to think she was inviting anything.

His eyes were filled with compassionate understanding as he casually changed the subject. "I just had an idea. If you're not busy this morning, how would you like to go apartment hunting?"

"I'd love to! I never have anything to do but answer the phone." As though on cue, the telephone rang. Bliss made a face.

"Would you like me to get that?" Hunter asked.

"I'd really appreciate it." She started toward the bedroom. "I'll comb my hair and be right with you."

He got rid of someone who wanted to use her name for an obscure charity, then disposed of two other self-serving calls. As he was opening the newspaper to the classified section the phone rang again. Annoyed, he barked out a curt greeting.

"Hunter, baby, I've been waiting to hear from you," Clay Dennison's voice greeted him.

"I said I'd let you know," he answered shortly. "I just got here."

"I know what a fast worker you are. I didn't interrupt anything, did I?"

"What the hell is that supposed to mean?"

"Just a joke, don't blow your stack. How's it going with the girl?"

"It's all settled."

"I knew you could do it! You're a sweetheart."

"Yeah, I'm a real nice guy," Hunter drawled.

"Don't start having an attack of conscience," Clay warned. "Our deal is like lox and bagels. One's no good without the other."

"And you don't get *her* name on a contract until I get *yours*," Hunter answered grimly.

"Do you think I'd try to weasel out of our deal?" the other man asked in an aggrieved voice.

"You already know what I think," Hunter replied contemptuously.

A flush of anger mottled Dennison's cheekbones. "Okay, so I use people to get what I want. Are you so different, buddy boy?"

Hunter's knuckles were white as he cradled the receiver without answering.

Chapter Two

Bliss returned to the living room after combing her hair and touching up her makeup.

"I heard the phone ringing off the hook," she remarked. "It's heavenly to have someone else to deal with it."

"Every nut and bolt in the country seems to know where you are," Hunter commented. "But you won't have to put up with it much longer. When you're installed in your own apartment we'll get you an answering machine."

"What's that?"

"A gadget that takes messages. It's invaluable. You can ignore the ones you're not interested in."

"I can't believe all the modern technology you have here," she marveled. "I've seen ads in the newspaper for things I've never even heard of. What's a camcorder? Or a fax machine?"

"I'll bring you up-to-date in due time, but let's take first things first. Your top priority right now is an apartment."

"I'm ready when you are."

He had circled several ads in the classified section, which he handed to her. "We'll check out these places for starters."

While they waited for Hunter's car to be brought around, Bliss tried to decipher the newspaper shorthand: 1 bdr., cpts./drps., lg. sol., w/d. She puzzled over the unfamiliar terms as he guided her into a powerful, low-slung car.

"This must be carpets and drapes, but what does the rest of it mean?"

He looked where she was pointing before putting the car into gear. "Large solarium, which is probably a porch. People who compose those ads are the creative writers of our day. Just hope the washer/dryer is in working condition."

Bliss continued to read as he turned onto Wilshire Boulevard and merged with the traffic. "What do these numbers mean?"

"That's the rent."

"You have to be joking!" She gasped.

"Some of them are too good to be true, but we'll check them out, anyway."

She stared at him in disbelief. "You mean people actually pay this kind of money for *rent*? I could buy a whole herd of cattle for less!"

"Not here." He smiled at her perturbed expression. "You're suffering from culture shock, but you'll get over it."

"I doubt it. What am I going to do, Hunter? I can't afford these prices."

"Sure you can. You'll be rolling in money after you sign the contract." When she continued to look upset he said soothingly, "Trust me, honey, you'll be okay."

Strangely enough, Bliss did trust him. There was something very reassuring about Hunter. She sensed that he would be a good friend. Any other relationship between them would be a different matter, however. A little shiver ran up her spine as she remembered the predatory-male expression she'd glimpsed briefly. He'd even told her not to be too trusting. Was he warning her against himself?

Her troubling thoughts were pushed aside in the excitement of looking at apartments, although they weren't very promising. Some were old and run-down, in spite of the high rents. Others were little cubbyholes in modern buildings that were depressingly uniform. They gave Bliss claustrophobia.

"Don't get discouraged," Hunter advised. "We'll keep at it. You can't expect to find something the first day."

But they did. The next address on their list was a pleasant neighborhood in West Hollywood. Among the small houses and unassuming apartment buildings was a bungalow court built in a U shape. The architecture was old-fashioned, but an umbrella table and chairs in the central patio looked inviting, and pots of scarlet geraniums lent festive splashes of color.

A young woman was reading a newspaper under the striped umbrella. She was very exotic-looking, with long, straight black hair tied back with a red scarf. As Bliss and Hunter started up the walk she stood, displaying a truly magnificent figure. Her black leotard showed off every curve. Looking at Hunter rather than Bliss, she moved toward them with a dancer's grace.

His gaze held subtle male appreciation, but his voice was neutral. "Can you tell us where to find the manager?"

"If it's about the apartment, I can help you. I'm Shelley Calhoun. I own this place."

Hunter's nod acknowledged the introduction, but he didn't give his name or Bliss's. "Could we take a look at it?"

Shelley glanced past them to the sleek red Ferrari parked at the curb. Her gaze returned to inspect their casually elegant clothing. "Are you sure you read the ad right? It's just a small one-bedroom apartment, nothing fancy."

"I understand. May we see it?" Hunter repeated.

"It's still occupied. The present tenant is moving, but she won't mind showing it to you." She started toward one of the bungalows, saying over her shoulder, "You'll have to make some allowances. Mrs. Draper is quite elderly, and she can't live alone anymore. She's moving to a retirement home. The place is a bit of a mess, but I plan to have it cleaned up and painted when she moves out."

A small, frail woman answered her knock. She echoed Shelley's apologies about the condition of the apartment. "I'm trying to get things ready for the movers, but I don't seem to be making much headway." She looked around helplessly.

The living room was cluttered with the memorabilia of a lifetime. Photographs in large and small frames sat on every available surface, along with houseplants in various stages of health, souvenir ashtrays from resort hotels, cents-off coupons—an eclectic mixture of the past and the present.

After the initial shock, Bliss liked what she saw. The living room would be cozy when it wasn't so crowded, and sheer panels on the windows would give an airier feeling rather than the heavy drapes there now. The view of the patio would be very attractive.

"May I see the rest of the apartment?" she asked.

Hunter was regarding her with incredulity, but he followed along as Mrs. Draper showed them the bedroom, bath and compact kitchen.

When she'd finished the tour, Bliss announced, "I'll take it."

"I think we'd better talk about this first." Hunter took her arm and led her to the door. "Will you excuse us for a minute?" he asked Shelley.

She shrugged. "Sure, but if you think you want the place you'd better make up your mind fast. Several people are interested in it."

Bliss was silent until they reached the car. "We'd better grab it before someone else does," she told Hunter with a worried expression when they were out of earshot.

He shook his head indulgently. "My dear little Bliss, you really need someone to take care of you. Don't you know when you're being hustled?"

"Well, it could be the truth," she said defensively.

"People standing in line for that dump?"

"It's not as bad as it looks now. Once it's cleaned up and I get new slip covers for the furniture, it could be quite charming. Besides, it's the cheapest place we've seen."

"You don't have to watch your money that closely. You can afford something better than this."

Having made up her mind, Bliss felt the need to justify her choice. "I don't know where *you* live, but this apartment is more luxury than I'm used to, even before the island.''

Hunter masked his sudden rush of sympathy, knowing she'd reject it as pity. ''You're the one who's going to live here, so if you're pleased, that's all that matters. The only thing I would suggest is that you try to rent it on a month-to-month basis, in case you do change your mind.''

''I won't have to pay in advance, will I?''

He nodded. ''The first month's rent and a security deposit, or the first and last month's rent if she insists on a lease.''

Bliss's shoulders slumped dejectedly. ''We've just been wasting our time, then. I can't afford *anything* until I sign the contract.''

''No problem. I'll advance you the money.''

''I couldn't ask you to do that.''

''You didn't. I offered.''

She looked doubtful. ''It's an awful lot of money.''

He gazed at her searchingly for a long moment with something like regret in his eyes. ''In a shorter time than you imagine, you're going to feel a lot differently about money—and everything else.''

''I must seem hopelessly naive to you. I'm glad you think I can change.''

His smile was a little twisted. ''*Glad* isn't the word I would use.''

The landlady strolled down the path toward them. ''Have you made up your mind yet?''

''Yes, I'll take it,'' Bliss said eagerly. ''When can I move in?''

''Mrs. Draper will be out in a week, then figure another week to paint the place and give it a good cleaning. You can move in two weeks from today.''

"Not before then?" Bliss's face mirrored her disappointment.

"I don't see how. It will take that long to do a thorough cleaning job. You saw the condition it's in."

"Two weeks isn't so long," Hunter consoled her.

"Do you have to move out of your present apartment?" Shelley asked.

"I'm staying in a hotel," Bliss answered.

"That *is* rough. Well, I'll do what I can, but don't count on getting in any sooner." Shelley looked from one to the other, unable to hide her curiosity. "It's none of my business as long as you pay the rent, but is the apartment for you alone, or are you both planning on living here?"

"No, certainly not!" Bliss exclaimed.

Hunter tried to conceal his amusement at her heightened color. "Miss Goodwin won't be sharing it with anyone."

Shelley frowned slightly as the name rang a bell. Her mouth dropped open when she studied Bliss and made the connection. "You're the one who was on the deserted island!"

"Yes, but I'd appreciate it if you didn't tell anyone," Bliss said apprehensively.

"Okay, if you say so, but that's a hard thing to keep quiet. You're a celebrity."

"She doesn't enjoy the limelight," Hunter explained.

"What are you doing in *this* town?" Shelley asked.

Bliss sighed. "Sometimes I wonder."

Bliss felt like a new woman. Her immediate problems were solved, and she didn't feel as alone in an alien world any longer. Although Hunter stood to gain by helping her, she didn't think that was his sole motivation. Underneath his sophistication and cynicism, he seemed like a compassionate man. His behavior toward women he was sexually attracted to might be a different story, but that wasn't the case with her, anyway.

In the days that followed, Hunter proved that he wasn't motivated solely by self-interest. He drove Bliss around the city to give her some idea of its diversity, and took her to fancy places for lunch and dinner. All without making anything that could even remotely be considered a pass.

He introduced her to a fast-paced world she hadn't dreamed existed. Bliss was beginning to realize that Hunter was a very important man in Hollywood. The preferential treatment they received everywhere was because of him. Her own presence caused a minor flurry, but the steady procession of people came over to their table to talk to Hunter.

He also acted as her agent with Clay Dennison, obtaining what seemed like a fortune to Bliss.

The studio chief indicated it was more than he expected to pay. "Are you sure you don't want any other perks?" he asked with sardonic humor. "Maybe stock in the company?"

Hunter stared at him consideringly. "There *is* something else, now that you mention it. Bliss will need transportation. A new car would make a nice bonus."

"With the deal you just swung, she can buy her own car."

"Come on, Clay, I'm not talking about anything fancy, just wheels to take her around."

"I suppose I'd better give in before you change your mind and ask for a Rolls," Dennison said with a touch of acid.

By the time they left his office, Hunter had won every point. "You ought to negotiate for the United Nations," Bliss marveled. "We'd end up owning the world."

"With the shape it's in, that might be a liability," he noted.

"I can't believe the network is actually going to buy me a car."

"It's a small price for signing you up. I wonder if I could have gotten anything else out of him," Hunter speculated.

"I'm glad you didn't try. I was terrified that he might back out of the deal entirely."

"Not while you're such a hot property. To be perfectly honest, another network might have given you a better offer."

"I don't want to be auctioned off like a prize bull."

"Don't worry, you're the wrong gender," he said dryly.

"You know what I mean. Besides, Mr. Dennison's offer was very generous."

"With an attitude like that, you're going to get eaten alive in this town."

Bliss smiled enchantingly. "Not with you to take care of me."

Hunter didn't return her smile. He stared broodingly at her lovely, ingenuous face for a moment before muttering under his breath, "How did I let myself be talked into this?"

"I was just joking," she said uncertainly, her laughter fading. "I don't expect you to do any more for me than you've already done."

His mood vanished as swiftly as it had appeared. "Oh, I get it. You don't want anything more to do with me now that you're a rich woman. Okay, let's go shopping for a car and complete your independence."

Bliss would probably have bought the small white convertible even if she'd had to pay for it herself. It was love at first sight.

"Why don't you take it for a spin around the block?" the salesman urged, scenting a sale.

"Could I?" she exclaimed eagerly.

Hunter didn't share either one's enthusiasm. "Are you sure you can manage in traffic? Maybe I'd better drive you to a quiet neighborhood where you can get the feel of the car first."

"That won't be necessary," she said impatiently. "I've been driving since I was thirteen."

"But not in Los Angeles. Not in six lanes of cars."

"If I can miss an elephant, I'm not likely to hit a car."

"Why doesn't that make me feel any better?" Hunter mumbled as he reluctantly got into the passenger seat next to her.

Bliss inhaled the new-car smell of the tan leather seats and admired the walnut paneling, barely listening to the salesman explain the diverse features of the automobile. Halfway through his speech she turned the ignition key, moved the gearshift—and shot backward at top speed.

Hunter jammed on the brake, bringing the car to a halt before they hit the wall. "I though you said you knew how to drive," he said when he could talk.

"I *do*! That's where low gear is on my Jeep. How was I supposed to know this thing is backward?"

He appeared to be counting to ten. "Maybe we should look for a Jeep for you—or a tank. That might be a better idea."

"You don't have to be sarcastic. Anyone can make a mistake. Just show me how to put it into drive."

"You see those letters? *R* is for Reverse. Forget that one," he said hastily. "*D* for Drive is the one you want."

Her second attempt went better, although Hunter wasn't reassured. His long body was rigid as she drove out onto the street.

Everything went well at first. Bliss was too busy getting acquainted with all the interesting gadgets on the dashboard to do anything but stay docilely in her own lane. She soon grew bolder and chafed at a slow bus in front of her. As Hunter was starting to relax she zipped into the rapidly closing space between a taxi and a truck in the next lane. The cabdriver went predictably wild, shouting and leaning on his horn.

Bliss ignored him. "This car has great maneuverability," she remarked happily. "I'm going to enjoy driving it."

"For as long as you live, that is." Hunter drew a deep breath. "Listen to me carefully, Bliss. Remember when I told you a car is a necessity in L.A.? Well, I lied. You can get anywhere you want to go in a taxi, which is what I strongly suggest."

She glanced at his set face. "I didn't realize you were this nervous."

"It's a normal reaction when my life is in danger." He braced his feet against the floorboard as she switched lanes again. "You're supposed to use your turn indicator."

"What's that?"

"The lever on the steering wheel."

She flipped a lever and water squirted onto the windshield, momentarily obscuring her vision. "Why did you want me to do that?" she asked with a puzzled expression.

"I didn't mean...you pushed the wrong..." He closed his eyes briefly. "Pull over to the curb and stop the car," he ordered in a voice that brooked no argument.

"I only did what you told me to," she grumbled, following instructions. When Hunter opened the car door she looked at him in surprise. "Are you leaving me here?"

"Don't tempt me." He walked around to the driver's side and said, "Move over."

"I didn't think you were one of those macho men who make fun of women drivers," she complained as she slid over to the passenger seat.

"Believe me, there is nothing funny about your driving," he answered grimly. "Tomorrow I'm taking you far out in the country for a lesson in urban survival."

She grinned suddenly. "Yours or mine?"

He returned the smile reluctantly. "Yours, naturally. You don't think I'd be crazy enough to get in a car with you again?"

After all the papers had been signed transferring the car to her, Hunter took Bliss to the Polo Lounge at the Beverly Hills Hotel to celebrate. The leather banquettes were filled with glamorous, expensively dressed people who all seemed to know one another. The ones who weren't visiting back and forth were talking on telephones plugged into their booths.

The captain greeted Hunter by name and seated them immediately, ignoring a couple who were gazing in awe at the patrons. Bliss wasn't knowledgeable enough about television to recognize the two top stars of an evening soap opera the tourists were whispering about.

When they were seated she said to Hunter, "Who are all these people phoning?"

"Their bookies in a lot of cases, or maybe their agents, although they're hoping everyone will think they're discussing a big film deal."

She shook her head. "This is a very weird place."

"They don't call it La La Land for nothing."

"Someone should write an instruction booklet for newcomers."

"You're doing okay without one."

"I'm glad you think so," she answered wryly. "Most of the time I feel like an alien from outer space."

"I'm sure minor things must seem strange to you, but you've taken charge of your life with surprising self-reliance."

"That was out of necessity. I have to make my own decisions, good or bad. I don't want anyone else to do it for me."

He covered her fingers with his big hand. "I'd like to help."

"You have. I don't know what I would have done without you. Everybody else wanted to take advantage of my inexperience. You were the only one who wasn't motivated by selfish interest."

Hunter removed his hand and curled it into a fist. "I haven't been completely selfless, Bliss. You know I'm going to produce your story."

"You could get other work. I got the feeling in Mr. Dennison's office today that he was as anxious to get you as he was to sign me."

"I wouldn't say that," he answered carefully. "You just have to know how to handle these people. It's summed up in a saying—'Never let them see you sweat.'

If they think you're not interested, they shower you with offers.''

"First you have to have talent, though.''

"It helps not to fall on your face too often, but that's not difficult as long as you turn out the formula drivel Dennison and his ilk want."

"You're not too crazy about him, are you?''

Hunter shrugged. "He's no better or worse than the others. We're going to have a fight on our hands to make a docudrama that has even a glimmering of the truth, so be prepared.''

"You can do it," she said simply. "I think you can do anything you really want to."

Hunter's face was a study in conflicting emotions. Before he could respond, a man came over to their table. His navy silk shirt was unbuttoned to his breastbone, and the cuffs were turned back, revealing a gold watch on one wrist and a thick, gold link bracelet on the other.

"Congratulations, Hunter, baby," he said. "I hear you're making a comeback with a biggie."

"I wasn't aware of having been away," Hunter replied evenly.

"Don't take it like that, pal. I just meant you've been out of action for a while. You sure know how to pick your shots, though. The castaway flick will clobber the competition. I wouldn't mind directing it, if our schedules don't conflict," the man said casually.

A beautiful blonde with a gorgeous figure slid into the booth next to Hunter and kissed him enthusiastically. "Hunter, darling! I hear we're going to be working together. Isn't it exciting? I couldn't be more thrilled!"

He frowned. "You've been signed for the lead? I wasn't informed."

"Well, I haven't actually signed the contract yet. Clay said you have final approval, but I figured that was only a technicality. We've done some good things together." Her smile was reminiscent.

"This guy is a sweetheart to work with." The man muscled his way back into the conversation. "Some directors resent the producer, but I always welcome Hunter's input."

A shadow of annoyance marred the blonde's perfect face. She pointedly ignored the other man, turning her full attention on Hunter. "Let's get together soon, love. I've got some ideas for a couple of scenes that are pure Emmy material. One is a moonlight swim in the buff—very tasteful, of course. I might have to use a few palm fronds in strategic places if the censors get moral on us, but it will still be dynamite. That shot in a promo will guarantee an audience."

Bliss made an inadvertent sound of dismay. The woman's desire to turn a tragic misadventure into some kind of lewd exhibition was nauseating. It wasn't much different from the tabloid's intention or the raunchy men's magazine. And Hunter wasn't objecting.

He turned with a concerned expression at her small exclamation. "Don't worry about it, Bliss. We'll work it out."

The blonde had barely glanced at her before, but now her interest sharpened. "You're Bliss Goodwin, aren't you?" Her eyes went over Bliss appraisingly.

Hunter made a belated introduction. "This is Mona Jensen."

"You'll have to tell me about your experiences so I can get a feel for the part," she said to Bliss.

"Some other time." Hunter put a bill on the table. "Right now we're late for an appointment."

As he stood, the man said, "Let's do lunch soon."

"That was a bad choice," Hunter remarked as they waited for his car to be brought around. "I should have remembered the Polo Lounge is always swarming with Hollywood characters."

"What difference does it make? I've already signed the contract," Bliss answered bitterly. "I couldn't get out of it now, anyway."

He didn't answer until they were driving out of the circular driveway. "What's bothering you, Bliss?"

"I trusted you," she erupted angrily.

"How have I let you down?"

"You said you would tell my story honestly."

"I told you I would do my best," he corrected. "Why are you having second thoughts before we even have anything down on paper?"

"I can tell what it will be like," she said scornfully. "You're not interested in the things I had to do to stay alive. All you care about is how much nudity you can cram in."

"You're wrong. I have great respect for your courage. That's what this movie will be about."

"Not if that woman has her way."

"She won't. I'm the producer, and it's my word that counts."

"Will you guarantee that she won't go prancing around in the water wearing only false eyelashes and a hibiscus bloom in her hair?" Bliss demanded.

He countered the question with one of his own. "Are you sure you want this drama to be accurate?"

"That's what I was foolishly counting on."

"You mean you never went swimming in the nude?"

"Of course I did. It was warm, and I only had the clothes I was shipwrecked in. They wouldn't have lasted very long if I hadn't conserved them."

"Then why are you upset about Mona doing a nude bathing scene?"

"Because she makes it sound so...sexy!" Bliss's color rose, and she avoided his eyes. "It wasn't like that at all."

A little smile played around his firm mouth. "That's a bit like the old question—if a tree falls in the forest and nobody is around to hear it, does it make a sound? You don't think you looked sexy because no one saw you."

"I didn't look like *her*," she mumbled.

His eyes scanned her slender body, adding to her discomfort. "I could make an educated guess that you looked more provocative."

"Not unless you need dark glasses and a white cane. Are you really going to give her the part?"

"You don't approve?"

"We're nothing alike," she answered evasively.

"Actually, Mona is a good choice. From a distance she could easily pass for you, except that her figure is a little more...uh...generous."

Bliss wondered if he was speaking from other than general observation. Was Mona really Clay Dennison's choice for the role—or Hunter's?

"How did she hear about the part so soon?" Bliss asked. "I only signed the contract this morning."

"You can bet Dennison put out the word five minutes after we left his office. He'll get all the publicity he can while you're still hot news."

"You mean after a while I won't be?" she asked hopefully.

"Sooner than you imagine."

"I can hardly wait!"

"Celebrity has its privileges." He turned his head to smile at her. "For one thing, it means never having to wait for a booth at the Polo Lounge."

"Big deal. I can always use a pay phone."

Hunter's prediction came true sooner than he expected. Bliss was replaced in the newspapers by a heroic stewardess who had averted a tragedy by talking a hijacker into giving up without a struggle.

The statuesque brunette's picture was on all over the front pages, and accounts of her exploit spilled over into succeeding pages. The press hyped the story for a week. During the same period, a sensational divorce trial between two superstars completed Bliss's eclipse. She was yesterday's news.

Her first indication was a note slipped under the door of her suite. It was from the hotel manager, requesting her to stop by his office. This was a departure in itself. He usually came to see *her*.

The man was courteous, but that didn't make his message any more palatable. Her suite would no longer be complimentary.

"Of course we'd be delighted to have you stay on as a paying guest," the manager said smoothly.

Bliss considered it. Her apartment would be ready in a week, so it seemed foolish to move to another hotel. As she was about to agree, prudence took over. "What is the rate?"

"Nine hundred dollars a night." When she stared at him in shock, he said, "That's for the suite, which as you know is quite deluxe. I could let you have a nice single room for a hundred and fifty."

"I . . . I'll think about it," she murmured faintly.

"I'll have to know by this afternoon," he said adamantly.

Bliss could think of only one solution. She went upstairs and called Shelley to explain that she needed the apartment immediately.

"Gee, that's tough," the other woman said sympathetically. "I wish I could help you, but the whole place is torn up."

"I don't care what it looks like."

"That's not the problem. I only wish it were! Mrs. Draper never complained about anything, so I didn't realize what shape the apartment was in. I had to call a plumber to do extensive repairs."

"I won't get in his way," Bliss promised. "I'll get out of the house early every morning. All I need is a place to sleep."

"You can't stay there. The water is cut off."

That stopped Bliss for a moment, but she was desperate. "I'll manage somehow."

"I can't let you do that. The Board of Health could slap me with a big fine."

"I wouldn't tell anyone," Bliss pleaded, but Shelley stood firm.

Bliss hung up disconsolately. Why was everything such a hassle? She'd have to move out of this horrifyingly expensive hotel, but where? And on what? Her slender shoulders were drooping as she answered the door when Hunter knocked a few moments later.

"Is that what you plan to wear to the beach?" he asked, eyeing her white pleated skirt and navy blouse. They had a date to go to Malibu.

With all the traumatic events of the morning, she'd forgotten. "I can't go. I have to pack up and move."

After she'd explained, Hunter said, "I'm not really surprised, although they could have given you a little more notice. You're not going to find anyplace decent that's much cheaper, though. Why don't you stay here? It's only for a week."

"It would cost more than a thousand dollars for the room alone, and that's not counting food and incidentals. I can't afford it."

"You aren't exactly broke," he reminded her.

"All I have are promises so far."

"I'll advance you the money if that's what you're worrying about."

"I'm already in your debt for hundreds of dollars. I can't take any more. What would happen if the network decided to back out of our deal now that I'm not newsworthy any longer?" She was practically wringing her hands. "I never should have borrowed from you in the first place."

"You're getting in a panic over nothing," he soothed, urging her down onto the couch. "The network can't back out because they signed a contract, and if I'm not worried about the money, why should you be?"

"I can't help it," she said miserably. "I won't feel secure until I have a check in my hands. How long do you think it will take?"

"Unfortunately these things don't exactly move with the speed of light. The legal department has to go over the contract, and then it has to go to accounting, with a few stops along the way."

"How long?" she persisted.

"At least a couple of weeks, if you're lucky." When she looked at him in silent dismay he stared back at her thoughtfully. "Your immediate concern is finding a place to stay temporarily. Is that correct?"

"Yes," she said with a sigh.

"Okay, your problem is solved. You can stay with me."

Her eyes widened. "I couldn't do that!"

Hunter grinned. "Don't look so shocked. I'm not asking you to share a room. I have a house in Holmby Hills."

"I still couldn't."

"Why not?"

"Well, I...you..." Her voice trailed off.

How could she explain that in the world she came from, men and women didn't live together without being related or married. Hunter would find that hilarious. It was a hopelessly outdated concept, but she was the daughter of a missionary, after all. Lifelong rules were hard to break.

"Come with me." He tugged her to her feet.

"Where?" she asked, holding back.

"I'm going to set your mind at rest."

Hunter drove down Sunset Boulevard, past clusters of chic boutiques and famous restaurants. Beyond the Beverly Hills Hotel the broad avenue was divided by a bridle path down the middle. Large mansions, many behind walls or grilled fences, lined both sides of the boulevard.

He turned right onto a winding street shaded by tall trees. The stately homes they passed were well separated from one another. All were set on at least an acre of ground; many had more than that.

The driveway Hunter turned into ended in a paved area in front of a long, low modern house. It was screened from the road by a high wall and tall shrubbery.

"Is this your house?" Bliss asked as he cut the motor.

"The bank lets me pretend it's mine."

"It's gorgeous, Hunter, but I still can't—"

He cut her off. "Don't make up your mind until I show you around."

The spacious entry hall stretched to the back of the house, permitting a glimpse of a lovely oval swimming pool gleaming in the distance like a beautiful gem set on green velvet.

Without showing her the opulent rooms that opened on either side of the hallway, Hunter led her outside to a terrace, which overlooked the grounds. Facing them on the other side of the swimming pool was a small but elegant guest house. Navy-and-white-striped draperies were looped back, affording a clear view of the comfortably furnished living room. When Hunter gave her a guided tour, Bliss discovered there were also two bedrooms, two baths and a complete kitchen.

She looked around with shining eyes. "This is utterly charming."

"It's yours if you want it—no strings attached."

It was the perfect solution. She wouldn't actually be living with Hunter. This was a separate house entirely. "I'll take you up on your generous offer if you're sure I won't be in the way," she said earnestly.

"Don't you think there's room enough here for both of us?" He waved an arm to include the spacious grounds.

She'd known native villages that were smaller. "You live here all alone?" she asked wonderingly.

His firm mouth curved in a smile. "Not completely."

Her cheeks warmed. What a dumb question! A man like Hunter would naturally have female companionship.

He was amused at her transparent thought. "Max is usually around, nagging me about something."

As though summoned, Max appeared on the terrace. "Why didn't you tell me you were bringing home company?" He scowled. "The house is a mess."

"Have you been watching soap operas again?" Hunter asked.

"I had to find out if Heather told Jake she knew about his affair with Cybil, the little tart who works in the D.A.'s office. It won't do him any good, though. The police are set to nab him for murdering Conrad, his former brother-in-law." Max stared critically across the pool at his employer. "Why don't you ever produce good stories like that?"

"Produce them? I can't even understand them." Hunter strolled toward him. "I'd like you to meet Miss Goodwin. She'll be our houseguest for a while."

Max glanced at her with increased interest. "That will be a pleasant change. His nibs isn't always stimulating company." He gave Hunter a significant look. "Should I make up the room next to yours?

Bliss was uncomfortably aware of the question's implication. Would she be sharing Hunter's room, or keeping up appearances by staying—nominally—in the guest room?

"That won't be necessary," Hunter answered blandly. "Miss Goodwin will be staying in the guest house."

Max's startled expression showed this wasn't a normal occurrence. "Are you trying to tell me something?"

"I just did." Hunter took Bliss's arm. "Come on, let's go back to the hotel and get your clothes."

Chapter Three

The hotel suite had always seemed impersonal, in spite of its spacious comfort, but Bliss felt instantly at home in Hunter's guest house. Was it because he was so near? She had come to depend on him too much, she realized soberly—and not only for rescue from predicaments.

She looked forward to the time they spent together. Hunter made everything fun, whether it was dinner in a fancy restaurant or a walk along the beach. There was more to it than that, however. When he held her hand or put his arm around her shoulders casually, she felt a breathless kind of excitement.

That was what worried Bliss. Hunter was a wildly attractive man, but it would be the worst kind of folly to fall in love with him. He'd be either amused or appalled. Except for a few flashes of male awareness in his eyes, he treated her like a kid sister.

As though to prove the point, he ran a finger down her nose playfully. "For a girl who had only one borrowed outfit a couple of weeks ago, I'd say you're well stocked now."

She glanced at the heap of clothes piled on the bed, and the rows of shoe boxes on the floor. "I made a mess of this room in short order, didn't I?"

"It looks lived in."

"By whom? *The Beverly Hillbillies*?"

He merely laughed. "Take your time getting settled. I have to make some phone calls. Come over to the house for a drink when you're through."

She found him in the den an hour later, still on the telephone. His long legs were stretched out and crossed at the ankles, and the phone was cradled on his shoulder so he could take notes on a legal-size pad of paper.

When she hesitated on the threshold he beckoned her in, cradling the mouthpiece against his chest. "Fix yourself a drink. I'll be through in a minute."

She went behind the well-stocked bar and made herself a very mild vodka and tonic. Liquor was another new experience for her, and she was wary of it. Even a small amount loosened her inhibitions.

By the time she'd finished making her drink, Hunter was off the phone. "Sorry you had to be your own bartender. Are you all settled in?"

"More or less." She'd hung everything out of sight hurriedly, wanting to get back to him. "It's a darling house. You could rent it out for a fortune."

He hesitated. "I think you're better off where you are, Bliss."

"I wasn't suggesting you rent it to *me*!" She was aghast that he thought she was hinting. "I was only joking."

"I did consider it, but it would put constraints on both of us."

Bliss averted her eyes in embarrassment at what he was telling her. Did Hunter and his girlfriends frolic nude through the estate during their mating rituals? If Mona Jensen was one of his playmates, that wasn't a bad guess.

"I'll be out of here as soon as possible," she murmured.

"Don't feel pressured. If you weren't welcome I wouldn't have extended the invitation."

Bliss was afraid she'd appeared ungrateful. "I only meant I'll try not to disrupt your life any more than necessary. I don't expect to be treated like a guest. Just pretend I'm not here."

Something flickered for an instant in his eyes. "That would be hard to do."

Max came into the room. "What would you like for dinner?" he asked Bliss.

"Whatever you'd planned will be fine," she assured him.

"I hadn't planned anything. The boss is going out tonight, so you can choose what you want."

"Oh, please don't bother to cook for me. I don't want to make extra work for you." She was rapidly feeling like excess baggage in this bachelor establishment.

Max eyed her dispassionately. "It's no more trouble to cook for two than one."

"I thought maybe you'd planned to go out, too," she said tentatively.

He gave her an incredulous look. "With the Dodgers on TV?"

"Max is a great chef," Hunter remarked. "I wish I were joining you."

"What's stopping you?" Max asked the question Bliss couldn't.

"I have an industry meeting." Hunter stood and put his glass on the bar. "If you'll excuse me, I have to change clothes."

"You want to come into the kitchen and take a look in the freezer?" Max asked Bliss.

She followed him, although her mind wasn't on food. Did Hunter really have a meeting, or was that just a polite excuse? Not that it was any of her business. Hadn't she told him to ignore her? It seemed to have been an unnecessary suggestion.

The large kitchen was a cook's dream, equipped with every gadget and labor-saving device. Next to the double-door refrigerator was a freezer crammed with enough food to stock a grocery store.

Max stood in front of the open door, peering in. "We have steaks, chops, spaghetti sauce, lasagna. What appeals to you?"

"Good Lord, you could open a restaurant," Bliss exclaimed.

"Don't think I didn't consider it when times were tough."

She smiled. "I heard a sad story like yours once. It was about a poor family. The master was poor, the butler was poor and the groundskeeper was poor."

"Okay, so we weren't scraping the barrel. But L.A.'s not your ordinary town. You got to keep up appearances here. I keep telling the boss that."

Bliss glanced through the window at the floodlit lawns bordered by carefully tended flower beds. "He must have been listening."

"Not him. He never would play the game."

"Then how did he get all this?"

"Talent still counts for something, but he could have been head of the network if he hadn't insisted on trying to make quality shows."

"Don't you admire him for his integrity? I certainly do."

"What do you think keeps me here through the bitter and the better?" Max slammed a carton of spaghetti sauce down on the counter. "It just fries me that those knuckleheads don't appreciate the boss."

"I don't think Hunter would enjoy being head of the network," Bliss said thoughtfully. "It must involve a lot of politics, which he'd hate."

"You've got *that* right." Max grinned. "It would sure make me king of the supermarket, though."

Max wouldn't let Bliss help with dinner, but she insisted on eating in the kitchen with him. She left soon afterward, knowing he wanted to watch the ball game.

It was still early, and a long, dull evening stretched ahead of her. She selected a book from Hunter's extensive library, trying to shake off a feeling of loneliness that was absurd, considering her present good fortune. She'd known what it was like to be *really* alone.

Television helped dispel the silence in the guest house, but it didn't hold her interest. She kept wondering what Hunter was doing—and who he was with. When that proved unproductive she took a shower and washed her hair.

After putting on a peach-colored satin nightgown with a delicate lace top, she got into bed with her book. The story was so engrossing that she barely heard the light tap on the sliding glass door in the living room. When it was repeated she jumped out of bed and raced to the closet for her peignoir. It could only be Hunter at the door!

The robe eluded her among the jumble of clothes she'd hung up so hastily that afternoon. Abandoning the search, she ran into the living room without it. Hunter's receding footsteps were already a muted sound on the flagstone.

She slid open the door. "Hunter, wait!"

He walked back. "I'm sorry. I didn't mean to wake you."

"I wasn't asleep. I was reading in bed. Did you want something?"

"Just to see if you were all right." His eyes flickered over her.

"Oh. Yes, I . . . I'm fine." She was abruptly aware of being very skimpily clad. The satin part of the gown was clinging yet not actually revealing, but the lace top left little to the imagination. Crossing her arms over her breasts she said, "If you'll wait a minute, I'll get my robe."

"Don't bother. I mean, I only stopped by to say goodnight."

"Did you have a nice time?" In spite of her discomfort, Bliss didn't want him to leave.

He shrugged. "These things come under the heading of a boring necessity. What did you do tonight?"

"Washed my hair and read a book I borrowed from you."

He gazed as the soft cloud of hair that curled around her bare shoulders. "It sounds as though your evening was as dull as mine. I was sorry to leave you alone on your first night here."

"I didn't mind."

After a short silence he said, "Well, I'll let you get back to your book."

That sounded pretty dull compared to his company. "I'm really tired of reading. Wouldn't you like to come in for a while." She looked up at him with unconscious seduction.

The moonlight made his eyes gleam in the darkness. "Are you sure that's what you want, Bliss?"

"Oh, yes! I can throw on a pair of jeans in two minutes."

Hunter's face was expressionless as he stared down at her. "On second thought, it's getting late," he said in a peculiarly flat tone. "I think I'll turn in."

Her sudden elation evaporated as she watched him stride away. It was nice of Hunter to come by to check on her, but it would have been nicer if he'd been interested enough to stay. Bliss would have been bewildered if she'd heard his muttered words to himself.

"Why the hell did I go over there?" Hunter yanked off his tie and flung it on the bed. "I've never yet put the make on an innocent who doesn't know the score." He stalked angrily around the room, taking off his clothes. "She doesn't even know what buttons she's pushing. The sooner I get her out of my life, the better off we'll both be!"

Bliss had the uncomfortable feeling that Hunter regretted his hospitable offer, in spite of his assurances to the contrary. He was so aloof the next morning that she rather expected him to make some excuse to get out of taking her to Marine World that day, as they'd planned.

She got her first inkling when Hunter called her on the house phone shortly before noon. That in itself was suspect. Why didn't he walk over? She was only a few steps away.

He didn't break the date, but his voice was remote. "I still have a few things to take care of in my office. I won't be able to leave for another hour."

"We can go some other time," she offered.

"I thought you wanted to see Marine World."

"I do, but you sound busy."

"I said I'd take you, and I will." He hung up.

Bliss was both hurt and irritated. The least he could do was try to be polite. A week's inconvenience wasn't such a big deal. She would have told him to forget the whole thing if she hadn't surmised it would lead to a quarrel. Hunter was spoiling for a fight.

She resolved not to give him an opening. So an hour later, while he maneuvered his way onto the Harbor Freeway she looked silently out the window, although there was nothing to see except streams of other cars.

"You're very quiet," he remarked eventually. "Is anything the matter?"

"No."

He glanced at her firm jawline. "I can tell *something* is wrong. What is it? I thought we'd solved all your problems."

"You did, and I'm very grateful to you," she answered primly. "I won't ever bother you with any more of them."

Hunter frowned. "Suppose you tell me what's bugging you. I don't intend to put up with an entire afternoon of sulky behavior."

"You don't have to *put up with me* at all! I offered to let you off the hook, but you chose to be a martyr instead."

"Will you tell me what the hell you're talking about?"

"Among other things, your insistence on keeping our date today when you didn't really want to."

"What gave you that idea?"

"Your whole attitude. It started last night."

He slanted a wary glance at her. "All I did was stop by to say good-night."

"Because you felt guilty about leaving me alone. I suppose that's when you started resenting me." She sighed. "I'm sorry if it bothers you to have me around. I'm not enjoying the situation any more than you are, but there's nothing I can do about it for a week."

After a deliberate pause, Hunter chose his words carefully. "I apologize for making you feel unwelcome, Bliss. That isn't the case at all. Something did occur last night, but I shouldn't have taken it out on you. I tend to overreact when I've made an error in judgment."

A weight lifted from her shoulders. Hunter's coolness wasn't directed at her. He was merely preoccupied because of something unpleasant that had happened at his meeting.

He turned his head to smile at her. "Shall we start the day all over again?"

From then on they were back on their old footing. Hunter was at his most charming, and the miles to Marine World flew by.

Bliss was fascinated by the huge tank filled with an endless variety of sea life. Large and small fish swam through the pale green water in a constant marathon, duplicating their activity in the ocean.

The ramps that wound around the multistoried tank were dimly lit to allow maximum viewing of the marine life. In the eerie light from the tank, spectators got almost the same feeling as a scuba diver in the deep.

Bliss stared through the glass, entranced. "Look at that grouper. And there's a big sea bass. The villagers used to celebrate when they caught one of those."

"Do you like to fish?"

She shrugged. "I got my fill of it on the island."

"I suppose that would have been an important food source," he mused. "But what did you use for gear? Did you salvage anything off the boat?"

"Nothing but the piece of wood I was clinging to, and a bait knife I grabbed at the last minute. To fight off sharks," she explained matter-of-factly.

"My God," he muttered under his breath.

"Fortunately I didn't run into any, but the knife certainly came in handy. That's how I was able to cut vines and a bamboo pole."

He was regarding her with awe. "What did you use for bait and a hook?"

"Everything was makeshift. You don't want to hear the details now," she said deprecatingly.

"Yes, I do. This is all material for the documentary."

Bliss was suddenly deflated. She'd thought his interest was in her, personally. "I make a hook out of a safety pin that was holding my jeans together." She smile sadly. "Mother would have made me sew on a button if she'd known. I used sand crabs and crayfish for bait, and I tied a stone to the vine for a sinker."

"You're really something else," Hunter said huskily. "I doubt if I could have done as well."

She forced back the sadness. "A big strapping fellow like you? You'd probably have built a yacht and sailed home."

"Did you ever think about making a raft and trying to get back to Africa?" he asked curiously.

"It occurred to me, of course, but I didn't have the material or the tools. And then there were storms and sharks to think about. Sometimes they circled the island for days at a time. I decided to take my chances on being rescued.''

"I'm glad you did," he said simply.

"I am, too," Bliss murmured. She'd never have met Hunter if she hadn't.

"Will it bother you to go back?"

She gave him a startled look. "Why would I do that?"

"We'll be doing some location shots there."

"Whatever for? It's simply a deserted island, too tiny to have a name."

"You've put it on the map. Everyone wants to see where you lived all that time." When she didn't answer immediately he said gently, "You don't have to come."

"Will you be going?"

"Yes, I want to make sure they don't turn it into a resort area."

"Then I guess I wouldn't mind," she said hesitantly.

"You don't have to decide now. We won't even start production for a couple of weeks."

"How soon will you need me to do whatever a consultant does?"

"As soon as we have a working script."

They were suddenly surrounded by an exuberant group of schoolchildren shepherded by a couple of harried teachers who kept trying to keep them in tow. Bliss and Hunter moved toward the exit to give them room.

The bright sunshine was dazzling after the underwater world inside. They put on sunglasses and strolled down to look at the tidal pools teeming with tiny fish and crustaceans. Bliss stared down at them, remembering when these creatures had meant survival. Maybe it had been a mistake to come here.

Hunter was watching her covertly. "Why don't we do the town tonight?" he asked casually. "Dinner, dancing, the works."

Her faint melancholy dissipated instantly. "Sounds terrific, if you'll bear with me. I haven't gone dancing since I was in college."

"Then I'd say you were long overdue."

Hunter took her to a place on the Sunset Strip where they received the deferential treatment she had grown to expect with him. Their table was on the edge of the dance floor, and the service was impeccable.

"You're right. Celebrity has its advantages," she remarked after the headwaiter and the wine steward had departed.

"Are you enjoying it?"

"I meant you, not me. My fame was fleeting, as you predicted."

"You can attract attention anonymously." He gazed at her with frank admiration.

She shook her head. "This town is filled with women a lot more glamorous. Only my funny name identifies me."

"I'm willing to dispute that, including the last part. Your name suits you."

"I never thought about it until I went to college and everybody made a big deal about it. I even thought it was kind of nice. My father explained that I'd made them blissfully happy. They were both over forty when I was born, and they'd given up hope of ever having a child."

"It should be a comfort to know they achieved their dream," he said quietly. "Not everyone does."

"I suppose so," she answered in a muted voice.

"Would you like to dance?" he asked.

Bliss would have preferred to watch, but she followed Hunter onto the dance floor. Everything else was driven out of her mind as she stiffened in his arms.

"Relax." He drew her close and smiled down at her. "This is a lot easier than fighting off sharks."

"Not really. I wouldn't have cared if I'd stepped on their feet."

His lips brushed her temple. "Sharks don't have feet."

"But you do," she said faintly.

They circled the floor silently for a few moments before he said, "You're a fraud."

"What?" She gave him a surprised look.

"You're as light as a cloud in my arms."

Even though she suspected it was a well-worn line, Bliss glowed with pleasure. The dates she'd had in college certainly hadn't been like this. Hunter's lean body left no doubt that it belonged to a man, not a boy. She ran her hand lightly over the supple muscles of his shoulders, sensing the power he could unleash.

"Are you having a good time?" he asked.

"The best ever. You're so good to me, Hunter," she said impulsively.

"That isn't difficult." He held her so close that she could feel the steady beat of his heart. "You're so sweet and unspoiled." As her pulse quickened he continued, "You deserve the best after what you've been through."

When would she learn? Bliss thought sadly. Every time she hoped Hunter was starting to care for her, it always turned out to be wishful thinking. He was merely sorry for her.

"I guess everybody goes through bad times," she remarked tonelessly.

He smoothed her hair tenderly. "Your troubles are all behind you."

"Are they?" Not if she continued to depend on Hunter for her happiness.

"Believe it." He guided her head onto his shoulder.

Bliss decided not to borrow trouble. Her life was full right now, so why not enjoy it?

The week went by much too swiftly. Hunter took her to a play one night and a movie another. During the day they went to the county fair and fed the fish in a pond in Beverly Hills, within sight of the posh boutiques.

A couple of times Hunter did have business to take care of, and Bliss was left on her own. Max found her weeding a flower bed on one of those afternoons.

"That's what we have a gardener for," he scolded. "You'll ruin your nails doing that."

"I can get new ones." She held up her hands to display ten perfectly polished ovals. "They're plastic."

"Most things in this town are, including the people," he commented cynically.

"Not Hunter," Bliss said softly. "He's twenty-four-carat gold."

"You're right about that." Max hesitated. "He's no phony, but he isn't a saint, either."

"Very few people are." She laughed. "You're talking to a missionary's daughter."

He gazed at her without expression, then asked suddenly, "How much longer are you going to be here?"

"Only two more days." Bliss had gotten accustomed to Max's abrupt manner, so she wasn't offended. "I hate to see the week end," she said wistfully. "It's been like a honeymoon." As soon as the words were out of her mouth, her cheeks turned scarlet. "I didn't mean we...Hunter never tried...it was just a figure of speech," she stammered.

Max was staring at her incredulously. "I can't believe what I'm hearing," he muttered under his breath. Finally he wheeled around and started back to the house, saying over his shoulder, "I've got some cookies in the oven."

Bliss was embarrassed by her slip of the tongue, but in another way she didn't regret it. Max's amazement that she and Hunter weren't sleeping together showed what he'd been thinking.

Max was lying in wait when Hunter returned later that afternoon. He attacked with his usual directness. "What kind of game are you playing with Bliss?"

Hunter frowned. "I don't know what you're talking about."

"She's in love with you, and you've been leading her on for kicks."

"Where did you get an insane notion like that? I never laid a finger on her."

"She told me that, too, or at least I got the picture. That's not your usual speed. Why are you turning on the charm if you're not interested in her?"

"I don't believe this," Hunter said incredulously. "Are you saying I'm a cad because I haven't slept with her?"

"Don't get noble with me. I'd be more impressed if you hadn't encouraged her to fall in love with you."

"She doesn't know what love is." Hunter's expression was bleak. "I'm the first man she happened to meet. It could have been anyone. At least I didn't take advantage of her."

"Not much you didn't! You spent all week making her feel like Miss America. How's she going to feel when you dump her?"

"I don't intend to dump her, as you so inelegantly put it," Hunter answered with dignity. "We'll continue to be friends, but Bliss needs to meet other men. She's too inexperienced right now to know what she wants."

"That's a cop-out!" Max's raised voice carried through the open windows, waking Bliss from a nap.

She was puzzled by what seemed to be an argument between the two men. They joked back and forth a lot, but it was always good-natured. This exchange didn't sound friendly.

Max was clearly disturbed. "You've been playing dirty pool, and now that the damage is done, you want to pretend it wasn't your fault."

"I didn't *do* anything!" Hunter shouted.

"That might ease your conscience, but it's no excuse. There's enough fair game out there. You didn't have to target a sitting duck."

"Okay, that's it! You're way out of line, Max." Hunter sounded ominous.

"So go ahead, fire me."

"I damn well might!"

The argument ended with a crash of slamming doors. Hunter stormed out of the room, and Max took out his wrath on the kitchen cabinets. Bliss hadn't been able to figure out what the quarrel was about, but she thought it prudent to stay away from both of them.

It was a full hour before Hunter came looking for her. He was still simmering, although he tried to be pleasant.

"What have you been doing all afternoon?" he asked.

"Oh, a little gardening and a lot of loafing," she answered brightly. "How was *your* day?"

"Just dandy," he answered through his teeth.

Hunter never complained to her, but Bliss knew he must have problems in his line of work. When the stakes were high, the pressure mounted. The last time he'd been in this kind of mood was after another business meeting, the night she arrived.

"You look tense," she remarked. "Would you like me to give you a back rub?"

"No! I mean, I'm not tense."

"Yes, you are, even if you won't admit it." She urged him into a sitting position on one of the chaises.

Hunter's shoulder and neck muscles were taut under her probing fingers. Gentleness wasn't going to accomplish anything. She slid her hands inside the neck of his jacket and kneaded the corded tendons firmly.

His long torso was rigid at first, but he relaxed under her rhythmic strokes. "Mmm, that feels good."

"I told you so." She slipped his jacket off. "Lie down on your stomach."

"I don't think—"

"Just do it." She gave him a little push and sat down on the chaise beside his prone form. "You need this."

"I need a psychiatrist," he muttered.

"You shouldn't let people bother you so much," she said soothingly. "You have to be true to yourself. As long as you know you're doing the right thing, that's all that matters."

"You're making this very hard for me, Bliss. I'm afraid I'm not being fair to you." He sat up abruptly.

"You don't have to keep up a front for me," she said softly. "I don't expect you to be Superman. Everyone has problems that make them testy now and then."

"How can I get through to you?" He groaned. "You're a babe in the woods, expecting every story to have a happy ending. Unfortunately it doesn't work that way. You don't get what you want in this world merely because you want it."

"I did," she answered simply.

"But that's just the point. You don't even know what you want yet."

"Yes, I do." Her eyes met his unwaveringly.

After a long pause, he said with uncharacteristic uncertainty, "Maybe it could work."

As they gazed at each other wordlessly, Max approached unnoticed. He plunked down a plate of hors d'oeuvres on a small table.

"Nice going, stud," he commented acidly. "I see you're still on a roll."

Hunter's bemused expression hardened as he turned it on the other man. "You'd make the Olympics if they had an event for jumping to conclusions."

"And you'd win the gold medal in *your* category." Max stalked back to the house.

Bliss sighed. He had effectively destroyed a very precious moment. Hunter was once more austere. He stood and put on his jacket.

"Would you mind going someplace casual for dinner?" he asked. "I'd like to turn in early tonight."

"We don't have to go out at all. Max can have the night off, and I'll fix something simple for us right here." That might be the best way of defusing the tension between the two men.

Her suggestion wasn't well received. "Don't make waves, Bliss." Hunter strode off.

The evening couldn't be called a success. Hunter's effort at conversation was just that—an effort. His thoughts were in some dark place that was a mystery to Bliss. They were both relieved when dinner was over.

Hunter apologized as he walked her to the guest house. "I'm afraid I wasn't very good company tonight. We'll do something special tomorrow night."

"That's all right. I enjoyed the dinner," she answered politely.

"Pizza and beer?" His mouth curved mockingly.

How could she explain that it didn't matter what they ate or where they went, as long as she could be with him? Bliss finally admitted what she could no longer deny. She was hopelessly in love with Hunter.

Forcing a smile she said, "It was a treat for me. Pizza was one of the things I used to dream about."

"For God's sake, stop being grateful!" Deep lines bracketed his mouth. "How many times do I have to tell you I don't want your gratitude?"

She ached for him as he stalked off. It was useless to tell herself that Hunter's behavior was boorish; she wasn't responsible for whatever was bothering him. But it was impossible to work up any righteous indignation. When someone you loved was in pain, you hurt, too.

Neither television nor her book diverted Bliss after Hunter left. Her mind kept wandering back to him. Finally at midnight she turned off the light in the hope that a good night's sleep would make them both feel better.

After tossing and turning restlessly she knew that sleep was out of the question, for her at least. She switched on the lamp again. While she was staring out the window, a solution occurred to her. Whenever she'd felt this depressed and restless on the island, a brisk swim had relaxed her enough to sleep. Her problems were even more complex now, but it was worth a try.

Since the main house was dark and the pool lights were on a timer that went off at midnight, Bliss didn't bother with a bathing suit. One of the few things she'd enjoyed during her ordeal was swimming in the nude.

The cool water was a shock at first, but she enjoyed the sensual feeling against her bare skin. An invigorating swim soon warmed her, and the physical exercise achieved the desired result. She frolicked as mindlessly as a fish, alternately swimming laps and diving deeply to glide along the bottom. Her tranquility was abruptly shattered, however, when she surfaced for air. Hunter's deep voice threw her into a panic.

"You look like a mermaid." He was standing by the edge of the pool watching her.

"What are you doing here?" She gasped. "I thought you went to bed."

"I did, but I couldn't sleep. When I heard you out here I decided to join you."

"No, don't! I . . . it's really too chilly for swimming."

"I can take it if you can. Besides, I like it cold." He dove cleanly off the side.

Bliss couldn't decide what to do. She hadn't even brought a robe outside. Should she make a dash for it while he was swimming? Or would it be better to wait and hope he'd only come out for a brief dip?

While she hesitated indecisively he surfaced beside her. "The water isn't cold, it's refreshing."

"At first. But it . . . uh . . . it gets nippy after you've been in for a while."

"That's because you're not swimming. Come on, I'll race you to the steps."

"No, you go ahead. I'm going to get out and dry off."

"Okay, I'll give you a boost." Before she could stop him, his hands grazed her hips as he reached for her waist. The awareness in his eyes was visible even in the dim light.

"I didn't think anybody would be around this late," she explained haltingly.

Hunter wasn't listening. His hands were skimming her rib cage, moving higher. "I was wrong. You're lovelier than a mermaid. Your body is as beautiful as I knew it would be."

She grabbed his forearms. "Let me go, Hunter."

He was too lost in the wonder of her body to hear her plea, much less comply. He continued to caress her cool skin, warming it from within. When he reached her breasts she dug her nails into his arms. The feeling of his fingers circling her rigid nipple was indescribable.

"I've dreamed about touching you like this," he murmured. "I imagined what it would be like, and you're all my dreams come true."

Bliss dimly realized she should stop him before it was too late, but she lacked the will. Hunter was arousing passions she'd never experienced until then. Her body was making demands that couldn't be denied.

"I've never wanted any woman this much." His voice was smoky with desire. "I've told myself to leave you alone, but you're in my blood." His mouth slid over her shoulder and across the curve of her breasts where they swelled above the water. "I want to know every exquisite inch of you."

She trembled as he gratified his wish, stroking her so intimately that she clasped her arms around his neck and twined both legs around one of his thighs to keep from sinking.

"You want me, too, don't you, my little love?" he asked triumphantly.

His mouth closed over hers, vanquishing any remaining doubts. When his tongue probed deeply she pressed closer, feeling excitement pulse through her veins.

The same urgency gripped Hunter. He hooked an arm under her legs and cradled her against his chest while he carried her up the ladder. She shivered when he set her gently on her feet, but not from cold.

Hunter didn't realize that powerful emotions were responsible. He picked up the towel he'd brought and wrapped it tenderly around her before lifting her again in his arms and carrying her into the guest house.

The bedroom was lit by the small reading lamp she'd left on. When he placed her on the bed and started to unwrap the towel, Bliss clutched at it.

"Turn off the light first," she whispered.

"You have nothing to hide." His tawny eyes blazed with almost primitive passion. "You're absolute perfection."

He knelt over her and stroked her legs, starting at her ankles and continuing up the length of her thighs. When his hands moved under the towel to touch her with arousing expertise, she turned her head away and uttered a choked cry.

"I know it's been a long time, sweetheart," he soothed. "I won't rush you. I want it to be wonderful for you." He eased the towel away and feathered her breasts with tantalizing kisses. "Tell me what pleases you."

"I don't know," she answered faintly.

"Don't be shy with me, darling." He cupped her cheek in his palm and eased her averted face back to his. "Look at me."

"Please, Hunter," she pleaded. "It's so difficult the first time."

A dead silence fell as he stared at her, the passion draining out of his face. "You're a virgin," he said in a flat tone of voice.

It was almost an accusation. "Is that so terrible?" she asked uncertainly.

"I should have known." He stood and glared down at her. "Why didn't you hold my head underwater when I made a pass out there?"

"Because I...I'd never felt..." She moistened her dry lips. "I wanted..."

"Listen to me, Miss Robinson Crusoe. I've done a lot of things for you, but there are limits. If you're looking for sex education, enroll in a course! I've never yet deflowered a virgin, and I'm not going to start with you."

He stormed out of the room, leaving her bewildered. Bliss wrapped herself in the towel and curled into a miserable little ball. What had happened to the tender lover who only wanted to give pleasure? Her body still remembered the touch of his hands and mouth. How could he leave her like this?

Anger joined confusion and misery as she realized why Hunter had walked out on her. He was only interested in women experienced enough to satisfy him, and she didn't qualify. No deeper feelings were involved on his part. She was just another warm body to him, one that wasn't worth the effort involved.

How could she have imagined herself in love with a man like that? Tomorrow she would move out of this house if she had to sleep in the bus station! Anything would be preferable to staying here and accepting his grudging charity.

Bliss continued to fuel her anger as a shield against the pain that refused to go away.

Chapter Four

Bliss didn't even try to go to sleep that night. She spent the remaining hours staring out at the blackness that matched her mood, willing the horrible night to end. When the sky began to lighten imperceptibly, she got up and packed her belongings. By the time the sun appeared on the horizon and the first sleepy birds were beginning to twitter, she was ready to leave.

It was too early to phone Shelley, so Bliss carried her things out to the car instead. She hated being grateful to Hunter for anything, but the little convertible was a blessing at this point. It meant she could leave his odious house without having to wait for a taxi—and, she hoped, without ever having to see him again.

What would his attitude be this morning? Restrained annoyance? Gritty-toothed endurance? Or would he be conciliatory and try to apologize? She doubted *that* very seriously. Hunter was a law unto himself. But whatever his mood, Bliss wasn't interested in finding out. Her only wish was to get him out of her life.

Loading the car didn't take long. It was still very early, but she couldn't wait any longer. She dialed Shelley's number and waited impatiently while it rang many times.

When the other woman finally answered in a voice thick with sleep, Bliss identified herself and said, "I know the apartment wasn't supposed to be ready until tomorrow, but I'm moving in today. I don't care if the plumber isn't finished, or the paint is still wet. It's only one day early, and I simply must have the apartment right away."

"Don't get manic. It's no problem." Shelley looked at the clock and groaned. "My God, it isn't even seven o'clock yet. Do you always get up this early?"

"No, I—" Bliss wasn't about to explain her sleepless night. "I'll be right over."

"Okay." Shelley sighed. "Stop by my unit and I'll give you the key."

Bliss felt as though a load had been lifted from her shoulders. She was finally free of Hunter! Her only remaining worry was running into him as she was leaving. What could they possibly say to each other? She'd thought of leaving a note thanking him for his hospitality, but after last night it would seem like mockery.

The main house was reassuringly silent when she left, but Bliss walked on the grass instead of the flagstone to avoid making any noise. She didn't breathe normally until Hunter's estate was a vanishing image in her rearview mirror.

Shelley was still in her robe when Bliss rang the doorbell. "Where were you when you phoned? Around the corner?" she asked with a lifted eyebrow.

"There wasn't much traffic," Bliss said uncomfortably. "I'm sorry I woke you so early. If you'll give me my key I won't bother you anymore."

"I'm up now, anyway." The other woman shrugged. "Come in for a cup of coffee. It's just about ready."

"I don't want to put you to any trouble."

Shelley grinned. "You already have. What was the big emergency? Did you get thrown out of the place where you were staying?"

"Not exactly. I . . . Something came up and I wanted to leave."

Shelley glanced curiously at her as she got cups and saucers out of one of the kitchen cupboards. "I tried to call you at the hotel yesterday, but they said you moved out. I was going to tell you the workmen would be done ahead of time, but the desk clerk said you didn't leave a forwarding address."

"I didn't want anyone to know where I'd gone. Everybody's been pestering me so much."

"You were lucky to find a place where nobody recognized you." Shelley paused expectantly. When Bliss didn't respond she persisted. "Were you staying with friends?"

"I don't have any friends here," Bliss answered tightly.

"How about that gorgeous hunk who was with you when you rented the apartment?"

"He's a—I guess you could call him a business associate."

"I'd sure like to get into your line of work. What do you do?"

Bliss didn't care to discuss her connection with Hunter and the network. "I'm a teacher," she said.

Shelley laughed. "I don't think you could teach *that* guy anything."

"Hunter—Mr. Lord and I are only casual acquaintances. He offered me temporary employment, and I accepted it because I need the money. We'll be having only the most fleeting contact, if any."

Bliss suddenly realized she'd have to see Hunter again, after all. The network would never let her out of her contract, and even if they could be persuaded, she'd be destitute without the money. Not to mention the sizable chunk she owed Hunter. What had seemed like good fortune at the time was really a trap. She was a puppet on a string being pulled by greedy, unprincipled men.

Shelley was staring at her. "Was that Hunter Lord, the producer?" When Bliss nodded numbly she said, "He's a legend around this town. Are you doing a movie for him?"

"No, I'm supposed to be a consultant on the docudrama they're doing about me."

"Fantastic! With an in like that you could have a career in show business."

"I don't want to be in show business," Bliss answered sharply. "The people I've met so far haven't impressed me with their integrity."

"I know what you mean. I used to be a dancer until I got tired of all the phony baloney. The big shots promise you anything to get you into bed, but the next morning it's 'bye-bye, baby.' That's why I saved my money and got out when I had a chance."

"What do you do now?"

"This bungalow court nets me a nice little sum, plus my own unit rent free. I also have an aerobics studio. Everybody is fitness crazy now, and it's sort of my old line of work. I have other instructors, but I lead the jazzercise classes.''

"What are those?'' Bliss asked curiously.

"Exercising to music. I keep forgetting you've been out of action for a long time.''

"I was never in this kind of world,'' Bliss replied somberly.

"It isn't so bad if you learn not to trust anything a guy tells you—and then enroll in a few judo classes for insurance.'' Shelley smiled.

"You make it sound like a war between the sexes.''

"Now you've got it.''

"I can't accept that! What about loving and caring? In the world I came from, if someone showed compassion you could believe he was really sincere. Everyone here has an ulterior motive. It's a bigger jungle than the one I'm used to.''

Bliss had revealed more than she realized. Looking at her lovely flushed face, Shelley hesitated. "I didn't mean to say *all* men are rotten, but some are more...unobtainable than others. Women a lot more experienced than you have stalked Hunter Lord without even winging him. You'll do better picking someone who isn't such a challenge.''

"I wasn't speaking personally, and I'm certainly not looking for a man,'' Bliss answered stiffly. "But if I were, he wouldn't be in the top one hundred. May I have my key? I'd like to get unpacked.''

Shelley watched Bliss's straight back as she walked across the courtyard. Scooping up the black-and-white cat that twined around her ankles she said, "Poor kid. It's too bad she started at the top. A climber has to practice before she'd ready for the Matterhorn.'' She looked sternly at the cat. "You males are rotten to the core, do you know that, Casey?"

Bliss was busy at first getting settled in her apartment. There were so many details to take care of, like arranging for telephone service and having the gas and electricity turned on. The apartment was furnished, but that didn't include linens or kitchen equipment, so she had to shop for those items.

Money was a constant worry, although Bliss discovered that all the stores were happy to extend credit. Her name was still magic. It was the day-to-day expenses that were a problem—food, dry cleaning, gasoline, things like that.

Luckily Hunter had insisted on giving her some cash for incidentals. At the time she'd been reluctant to accept it, but now it was a godsend, even though every penny rubbed salt into the wound. She longed for the day she could pay him back with interest.

Bliss was lining dresser drawers one afternoon when the doorbell rang. Expecting a delivery, she went to the door. When she saw Hunter on the doorstep, her heart started to pound. She had imagined he'd be repulsive to her, but he was as devastatingly handsome as ever and even more virile. They stared silently at each other for a long moment.

Finally he said, "I figured this was where you went."

"What are you doing here?" she demanded.

"I was worried about you."

"I'm not going to run out on the money I owe you," she said witheringly.

"You know I don't give a damn about that."

"Oh, really? What other reason would bring you here?"

"Please, Bliss, I want to talk to you."

"That's unfortunate, because I don't want to talk to you ever again!"

"I know you're hurt, but I'd like a chance to explain. May I come in?"

A next-door neighbor came out to water her petunias. When the woman stared curiously at them, Bliss said grudgingly, "All right, but only for five minutes."

She pointedly didn't ask him to sit down, wanting him to understand that she meant what she'd said. Hunter was too disturbing to her peace of mind, but he mustn't know that.

He came right to the point. "First I want to apologize for the other night."

"I don't want to talk about that," she flared.

"We can't simply pretend it never happened."

She lifted her chin. "That's exactly what I've done. The incident was too unimportant to dwell on."

"That could easily be true with a lot of other women, but you're different."

"Yes, I know. Meeting an honest-to-goodness virgin certainly threw *you* into a panic. They must be as rare as chastity belts in this town—and just about as popular."

"I don't blame you for being angry, but—"

"Don't flatter yourself," she snapped. "I'm eternally grateful that nothing happened between us."

"I realized you would be," he said quietly.

The nerve of the man! Taking credit for doing a good deed after the way he'd lashed out at her that humiliating night. She couldn't let him get away with that.

"I'm supposed to believe you were overcome by nobility? Why don't you just admit you were annoyed when you found out I was too inexperienced to satisfy you?" Her cheeks were pink with outrage.

He stared at her in amazement. "Is that what you thought?"

"It's the truth."

"Nothing could be *farther* from the truth. You must have known I've been attracted to you from the start."

"Because you did some favors for me? That was merely good business. How much of a bonus did Mr. Dennison promise you if I cooperated?" From the suddenly guarded expression on Hunter's face, Bliss was miserably certain she was correct, although he denied it.

"Clay Dennison doesn't tell me what to do. I'm an independent producer, not one of his gofers."

"Would you have been as helpful if you hadn't wanted to produce my story?"

"To be perfectly candid, Bliss, I don't give a damn about doing your story. I'll give it every bit of my expertise, but I didn't ask for the job, and I don't much want it."

"Thanks a lot! It's nice to know my life doesn't interest you any more than I do."

He sighed. "You're determined to misunderstand everything I say."

"What difference does it make?" She felt suddenly defeated. "Your five minutes are up. Will you please leave?"

"Not until I explain why I acted as I did the other night. No, don't interrupt," he said firmly when she opened her mouth. "You're a very beautiful woman, Bliss, with an added dimension of shy delight in all the things everyone else takes for granted. I enjoyed our time together, and I would have enjoyed making love to you. If you'd been a normal woman I would have."

"I *am* normal," she cut in indignantly.

A smile relieved the strain on his face. "That was a poor choice of words, although you're way above average. What I meant was, you've led a sheltered life. Morals in today's world are very relaxed. People fall in and out of bed with partners they hardly know."

"Maybe I am old-fashioned, but I can't say I admire your life-style," she said with distaste.

"I wasn't speaking personally. I don't pretend to be a saint, but I've never been promiscuous. I have to care about a woman before I can make love to her."

That really hurt! "What made you suspend your rules for me? The only thing that stopped you was my beginner's status. I gather you don't give lessons," she said bitterly.

"I'm only glad I found out in time." His voice was gentle. "What almost happened would have been a terrible mistake. You would have regretted it afterward, and I would never have forgiven myself for seducing you." When she gave him a startled look he said, "Yes, Bliss, it would have been seduction. I made you aware of the pleasure your body can feel. You'd never been touched the way I touched you."

"Please don't," she begged in a choked voice.

The memory of those enflaming moments was agonizing. She'd tried to forget the erotic caresses that had turned her liquid with desire, but it was no use. One glimpse of Hunter's long, lean body renewed his spell. She was afraid to look at him for fear he'd guess the effect he was having on her, even now.

His eyes were compassionate as he gazed at her downcast lashes. "Human sexuality isn't anything to be ashamed of, Bliss. It can be beautiful and fulfilling, too precious to waste on someone you don't care about."

How could she tell him she *did* care when the feeling obviously wasn't mutual? "I'll have to take your word for it," she murmured.

"Believe me. Some day you'll fall in love and you'll be glad you waited." When she simply nodded mutely, he said, "Are we friends again?"

"I suppose so." It seemed easier than arguing.

"I'm glad," he answered softly. "I've missed having you around."

With a determined effort, Bliss forced herself to appear composed. "I should imagine you'd be glad to get your house back."

"It hasn't been the same without you." His voice had a husky quality. As she gazed up at him uncertainly, Hunter seemed to realize he was sending the wrong signals. He glanced around the room. "You appear to be pretty well settled here."

"For the time being. I'd like to order slipcovers and get some new curtains, but that will have to wait until I get my check."

"I can give you an advance if you're short of cash."

"No, I don't want anything more from you." That sounded ungracious, so she said, "I mean, you've done enough."

"You need money to live on," he insisted. "Don't be stubborn."

"I won't take it, Hunter," she said adamantly. "If you want to do something for me, speed up my payment."

"I'll get on it right away," he promised. "I'd like you to report for work tomorrow, so the least the network can do is put you on the payroll."

"Are you ready to start shooting?"

"No, we don't have a script yet. What I want you to do is work with the writer I hired. His name is Roger Paradine."

"I don't have any writing ability," she protested.

"That's not what we want from you. Just tell him your experiences, what it was like on the island, that sort of thing. Roger is very competent, I think you'll like him. I hope so, anyway, because you'll be spending a lot of time with him."

Bliss had the distinct impression that Hunter was washing his hands of her. "I'll look forward to meeting him," she said coolly. "I haven't really met anyone here except you."

"I'm aware of that." His face was expressionless. "All that will change once you start to work."

"I can hardly wait," she said lightly.

He stared at her consideringly. "Roger might be just right for you. He's recently divorced, so he's available but not looking for a heavy commitment yet."

"Is that supposed to be a recommendation?"

"Definitely. You and he can have fun together without getting involved."

"He can't be much of a prize if that's his greatest asset."

"Don't jump to conclusions. I think you'll be pleasantly surprised."

Every added plaudit was another blow. Hunter was so eager to get rid of her that he was setting her up with other men. Well, if that was what he wanted, she'd play along.

"Okay, I'll keep an open mind," she promised. "Who knows? Maybe it will be love at first sight."

"You don't even know what love is at this point," he said tersely. "You need to go out with a lot of men before you have a glimmering."

"What you're really saying is, I should go out and get some experience," she replied scornfully.

"No! If I didn't have faith that you'd stick to your principles, I wouldn't let anyone near you."

"I don't need a bodyguard," she said angrily. "I'm an adult woman, capable of making up my own mind about what I want to do."

"You have the body of an adult, and the judgment of a child," he answered roughly.

She stiffened. "You've already made that point."

"I didn't come here to argue with you, Bliss." He sighed. "Whether you believe it or not, I have your best interests at heart."

"Of course your reward from Mr. Dennison has nothing to do with it?" The expression on his face was answer enough. She had to end the discussion before her last shred of pride was destroyed. "I didn't mean that," she said hastily. "I appreciate your concern, and I'll take your advice."

He stared at her moodily, not fully convinced. "I hope so. Just remember, I'm always here if you need me."

"I won't. I mean, everything's going to work out the way you want it to. Where do I go, and what time should I be there?"

After Hunter had given her directions, an awkward pause ensued. There didn't seem to be anything more to say,

"I think that about covers it," he said finally. "If you have any problems, give me a call."

"Thanks, but I don't anticipate any," she answered.

"I don't, either. Well... I'll see you when we start shooting, then."

"I guess so."

He seemed to have something more on his mind, but after a moment's indecision he merely said, "Take care, Bliss."

She felt like telling him it was too late for that, but she only nodded mutely.

Hunter's unsubtle attempt at matchmaking had left Bliss prepared to dislike Roger Paradine on sight. She was also on the lookout for signs that Hunter had tried to tout her to the other man in a like manner. If so, she intended to set the record straight speedily.

Roger was as tall as Hunter, without Hunter's powerful physique or intimidating sophistication. Roger was the boy-next-door type, tall and lanky, with pleasant features and a guileless manner.

Bliss liked what she saw, but that didn't mean she trusted him. If nothing else, Hunter had taught her that much. Her greeting was polite, yet reserved.

His was quite the opposite. "This is great! I've really been looking forward to meeting you."

"I hope you won't be disappointed," she answered evenly.

"I can't imagine that ever happening." He was gazing at her with open admiration, confirming Bliss's suspicions.

"Don't believe everything Hunter told you," she warned.

Roger laughed. "I can tell you haven't been in Hollywood very long. Around here the producer is always right."

"Or at least he thinks he is," she muttered.

"That's true, but Hunter is one of the good ones. I consider myself lucky to be working with him."

"How did you get the job?"

"We've done a few shows together before this one, and I guess he likes my writing."

"Are you friends outside of work?" She wanted to know how much was talent, and how much was Roger's willingness to make himself available.

"Not really friends, although I admire him tremendously. Hunter has a million acquaintances, but it's not easy to get close to him. I guess that's understandable in his position," Roger allowed. "Everybody has an ax to grind. That's the downside of the industry. You never know if people like you for yourself, or they just want to break in to show business."

"I'd find that very distasteful."

He shrugged. "It comes with the territory. Anyway, he's a great guy. But you've probably found that out already."

"My viewpoint is apt to be different from yours," she answered stonily.

He grinned. "Women are usually more enthusiastic than men."

"I'm not one of them."

His grin faded. "You don't like Hunter?"

"I'm sure he's everything you say he is. I barely know him. What I meant was, I'm not interested in *any* man at the moment." This was a good opportunity to get the point across.

"That will be good news to the male population. It means there's a chance for one of us lucky fellows," Roger said gallantly.

"I was simply stating a fact, not trying to be provocative."

After taking in her grim expression, he said gently, "You sound as though you've had a bad experience, too."

"Not like yours. Hunter mentioned that you were recently divorced."

He nodded. "Three months ago."

"I'm sorry," Bliss said automatically.

"Me, too." He jammed his hands in his pockets and strolled over to stare out the window. "I guess it was unrealistic to expect it to last."

"How can you say such a thing?" she protested. "Marriage is a sacred institution."

"Maybe in darkest Africa. Over here it's a way of getting another tax deduction."

"If that's your attitude, it's no wonder you two split up."

He turned to give her a twisted smile. "I figure if I can make a joke out of it, perhaps it won't hurt so much."

"I'm sorry," she repeated, really meaning it this time. "Would you like to talk about it?"

"What is there to say? Ours is a typical show business story. Deidre is an actress, and I'm a writer. Her work takes her all over—New York, London, Rome. I'm a screenwriter, so my work is here. We were apart more than we were together this last year."

"Couldn't you have arranged your schedules so you could have spent more time together?"

"It doesn't work that way. When I finished a script, she was usually in the middle of a picture. You can't hold up production because you want to be with your wife, especially when she's thousands of miles away."

"I see the difficulty," Bliss murmured.

"Our kind of arrangement is doomed from the beginning. No one with a grain of sense gets married here."

"I can understand your disillusionment, but you'll find somebody who's right for you. Millions of marriages survive a lot more serious problems than separation."

"Damn few in this town."

"You must know some happy couples," she persisted.

His somber expression lightened as he gazed at her distressed face. "Hunter told me you were naive."

Her soft mouth thinned. "Because I believe in love? That's just what I'd expect from him."

"He didn't mean it in a derogatory way," Roger soothed.

"I don't care *what* he thinks of me. I know people can be committed to each other. My own parents were living examples. They didn't have any of the things you people take for granted, but it didn't matter because they had each other."

"That's really nice." He was obviously placating her, but he managed to sound sincere. "Tell me about your parents. How did they decide to become missionaries?"

"It was after a trip they took to Africa. Dad was a well-known surgeon at the time, and Mother was a college professor. They were a little too old and too affluent to be called yuppies, but that was the life-style they led."

"My God! They gave all that up to go live in the bush? *Why?*"

"Because they wanted to help people on a more personal level. Everyone else on their safari was interested in seeing wild animals; my parents saw ignorance and illness that could be cured. They came home and sold everything. A month later we were living in a native village."

"They took you with them right at the start?"

"Of course. We were a close family."

"But you were just a child then. How could they subject you to living conditions like that?"

"I loved it." She smiled. "How many children get to wash their hair in a waterfall, or have monkeys and dik-diks for pets?"

"I'm almost afraid to ask, but what's a dik-dik?"

"A tiny deer, only twelve inches tall when it's fully grown. The babies are even more adorable."

In answer to Roger's questions, Bliss described life in the village and tribal customs. She told him about the patients her father had cured, and the schoolhouse the natives built for her mother. Reliving the past was a poignant experience. There had been so many good times. Hours went by as she talked, more to herself than to him.

Finally she stopped, a little embarrassed. "You must be bored to exhaustion."

"On the contrary. I'm fascinated."

"I'm afraid I got carried away, but this is the first chance I've had to tell the way it really was. So many people think of missionaries as religious zealots, but that wasn't true with my parents. They weren't fanatics. They simply wanted different things out of life."

"I wish I had a chance to know them," he said gravely.

She nodded wordlessly as a sense of loss gripped her. Forcing it back she said, "Well, we'd better get to work. Hunter would have a fit if he knew the time I've wasted."

Roger gave her a puzzled look. "What do you mean?"

"I was supposed to be telling you about the island."

"We'll cover that another day. I have more than enough material to get started on."

It was Bliss's turn to look confused. "But I haven't told you anything yet."

"You've given me wonderful stories. Your parents are as vivid in my mind as if I'd actually met them."

"What does that have to do with it? You're supposed to write about *me*."

"Your mother and father are part of the story."

"No!" She sprang to her feet. "I won't have you depicting them as some kind of crackpots! It's bad enough that I have to give up my own privacy, I won't let you invade theirs."

"Ridiculing your parents is the farthest thing from my mind. I admire them."

"You expect me to believe that after the way you tricked me?" she asked scornfully.

"How did I do that?" he asked in bewilderment.

"By asking all those questions, leading me on. I thought you were really interested."

"I *am* interested."

"In your paycheck." She started for the door. "I should have known you couldn't be trusted if you were a friend of Hunter's."

"Bliss, wait! I honestly thought you knew what he wanted."

"I do now, but it will snow in hell before he gets it." She slammed the door in his face.

On the drive home Bliss reviewed all the blistering things she was going to say to Hunter. This was one dirty trick too many! He knew how she felt about exposing her life to strangers. How could he think she'd allow her own parents to be victimized, too?

The car screeched to the curb with a squeal of brakes, and she was striding up the walk almost before the sound died away. Her eyes were flashing blue fire as she dialed Hunter's number. Max's voice did nothing to cool her temper.

"Let me speak to Hunter," she snapped.

"Bliss? Is that you? What's the good word?"

She gritted her teeth. "I can't think of one."

"What's the matter, kid? You sound like someone kicked sand in your face."

"More like hit me when I wasn't looking."

"Tell me who the crumb was and I'll flatten him."

"Please, Max, just put Hunter on the line."

After a surprised moment he said, "Sure, no problem." Max's bellow assaulted her ears as he summoned Hunter. "Phone call for you, boss. It's a beautiful woman."

Bliss could hear Hunter's voice as he called back, "I'm working. I can't talk to anyone right now."

"You don't know which one it is," Max shouted.

"I don't *care* who it is," Hunter yelled.

Bliss was seething. "Tell him he'd better talk to me because this is his last chance. I'm walking out."

"Why would you do a thing like that?" When his question met with stony silence, Max said, "Hang on, I'll go get him."

Hunter was working at an umbrella table strewn with papers. He glanced up with a scowl when Max approached with a cordless telephone. "I said I didn't want to be disturbed. If you need a hearing aid, I'll be happy to pay for one."

For once Max didn't rise to the bait. "It's Bliss. She sounds—"

Hunter didn't wait for him to finish. He grabbed the phone and said, "Hi, Bliss. How did your session with Roger go?"

"As well as you expected," she answered tautly. "He won't have any trouble with the first part of the script, and you can make up the rest."

"I don't understand."

"I'm quitting. Is that clear enough for you?"

"What happened? Did Roger say something to you?"

"It wasn't his fault. He thought you'd told me, but you're the big producer. You let him do your dirty work for you."

"Will you please tell me what the hell you're talking about?"

"Don't pretend you don't know. It's too late for that. Maybe I can't stop you from making the film, but it won't be an authorized version. I still own my own name, if nothing else."

"You won't even own that if you try to back out of your contract," he warned.

"So sue me," she answered scornfully.

"That's exactly what the network will do. Calm down and tell me what triggered all this?"

"I never agreed to have my parents' lives exposed to public view. I poured my heart out to Roger, and now he's going to write about all the intimate, funny moments I shared with two wonderful people." Her voice broke. "How could you do this to me, Hunter?"

"We have to talk," he said urgently. "Come over here and we'll straighten everything out."

"No! I don't ever want to see you again. And this time I mean it! You've sold me a lame elephant for the last time."

"Be reasonable, Bliss. You can't walk out."

"Watch me," she snapped.

"You're not thinking clearly. The network would put a lien on everything you own, besides getting a judgment that would take you a lifetime to pay off."

Cold reason began to seep through the heat of Bliss's anger. She'd be in a worse position that she was before—no money, no job and in crippling debt. Hunter wouldn't be there to lend a helping hand this time, nor would anyone else.

"We can't discuss this on the phone. Come over here," he coaxed. "I'd come to you, but I'm expecting an overseas call."

"Nothing you say will make me forgive you," she said uncertainly.

"We'll talk about it when you get here."

Max had listened shamelessly to the entire conversation. As Hunter cradled the receiver, he came out of the house.

"The kid's got spunk," he commented. "That was one thing I was worried about. She seemed almost too soft."

Hunter lifted one dark eyebrow. "You should have heard her on the phone just now."

"I did," Max answered calmly.

"Damn it, Max, one of these days you'll go too far. It's against the law to listen in on a private conversation."

"So sue me. Maybe you can get a group rate." Max picked up his employer's empty glass and disappeared into the house.

Chapter Five

Bliss's jaw was set pugnaciously when she rang Hunter's doorbell a short time later, but her defiance was mostly a front. They both knew he had won—as he always did—yet that didn't mean she had to make it easy for him.

Max opened the door and asked her in meekly. If he'd intended to make one of his outspoken remarks, a look at her set face changed his mind. "The boss is waiting for you" was all he said.

She marched through the house and out of the sliding glass door to the terrace where Hunter was once more engaged in paperwork. He stood to greet her.

Ignoring the storm signals in her glittering blue eyes he said mildly, "You made good time. Did your wheels touch down at any point?"

She didn't bother with preliminaries. "All right, I'm here. What excuse do you have? Not that I'd believe it, anyway."

"How can I explain if you've already stacked the deck against me?"

"That's what you've been doing to *me* since the day we met."

"Be fair, Bliss. It's true I advised you to sign the contract, but that was for—"

"If you say my own good one more time I'll push you into the pool!"

He smiled, which infuriated her more. "Can I take off my watch first? It was a gift that has a lot of meaning for me."

"What was it, an award for treachery?"

"I can't understand why you think I betrayed your trust. I'll admit I've done some things in my life that I'm not overly proud of, but not with you. Both my actions and intentions have been honorable where you're concerned."

Color swiftly stained Bliss's cheeks. He'd conveniently forgotten that shameful incident in the guest house. Was that his definition of honorable?

It wasn't hard to read her thoughts. "I've tried not to hurt you," he said softly.

She concentrated on the present. "You *have* hurt me, in the worst possible way. You knew I thought you were only going to film one incident in my life."

"Sit down, Bliss." He urged her gently into a chair. "You're well aware that we're doing this documentary because you're something of a curiosity right now. I don't like that any more than you do. I want people to know the courage and tenacity it took to stay alive on that island. Those qualities didn't suddenly appear out of nowhere. They were bred into you by two wonderful people who taught you to be strong and self-reliant. That's what I want to get across."

"But why must you go into such depth about my parents? The viewers will think they were weird for giving up a life of luxury. Roger certainly did."

"Even after he heard the whole story?"

"Well, no."

"Exactly. At the present time a lot of people think the way he did—negatively. They've seen cartoons of missionaries telling one another jokes in a huge kettle while cannibals dance around the fire."

"That's insulting!"

"Unfortunately the word conjures up that image."

"Mother and Dad weren't even missionaries in the strictest sense of the word. They were dedicated professionals who tried to make a little corner of the world a better place."

"Why don't you want people to know that?"

"I do!" She bit her lip uncertainly. "If I was absolutely *sure* . . ."

"You can be. Your job as a consultant is to see that the details are accurate. There won't be any Hollywood hype."

She wanted desperately to believe him, but Bliss knew how vulnerable she was where Hunter was concerned. He could convince her that the world was heart-shaped. Even now, with everything on her mind, she was tinglingly aware of him.

"You promise?" she asked slowly.

"I promise." He clasped her hands between both of his. "I want you to be happy."

She was fascinated by the changing color of his eyes. They were green and gold, like emeralds flecked with sunshine. The glow warmed the chilly feeling in her breast. Before the warmth could spread she drew a shaky breath and carefully extricated her hands.

"I'll settle for being satisfied," she said matter-of-factly.

His gaze was on the soft curve of her mouth. Without thinking he murmured, "I'd like to be the man responsible for that."

She jumped to her feet. "You know that's not what I mean."

He was more chagrined than she. "I didn't, either. I only meant I'll try to see that nothing upsets you."

His quick denial didn't make her feel any better. She turned away mumbling, "I have to go."

"Not yet." He caught her wrist. "Have I convinced you not to do anything rash?"

"Don't you always?" she asked bitterly.

He sighed. "I wish you were more comfortable about it."

"Even *your* power has limits."

"It would be nice if I were as omnipotent as you think." He stared at her moodily. "I'm as much a pawn as you are."

"Why are you making this documentary if you don't really want to?"

He shrugged. "It's what I do for a living."

"If I were unhappy with my profession, I'd get into a different one."

"I didn't say I disliked the industry. The quality films I've done have been very gratifying."

"What do you consider a quality film?" she challenged.

"One that makes people think and feel."

"I'd like to see some of the work you're proud of," she answered skeptically.

"Do you have an hour to spare? I just happen to have a cassette I could show you."

"You mean now?"

"Why not?"

"Don't you have work to do? You were snarling at Max earlier when he disturbed you."

Hunter laughed. "That's the only language he understands."

"Now you know what I have to put up with." Max's voice came wafting out of the den. "He gave me a kind word once, and I broke down and cried."

"Are you eavesdropping again?" Hunter demanded.

"Lucky for you. I've got the VCR all set up and ready to roll."

Hunter took her arm and led her into the house. "At least he's useful some of the time."

"That's the closest he gets to admitting he couldn't get along without me," Max told Bliss.

He had pulled the drapes in the den and opened the doors to the breakfront that held the VCR. Bliss half expected Max to watch with them, but he disappeared into the kitchen after they were seated on the couch.

She had a moment's feeling of incredulity. A short time ago she was vowing vengeance on Hunter, yet here they were, acting like old friends. Any second thoughts were driven from her mind, however, as soon as the film started.

The story was so engrossing that she was barely aware of Hunter, a rare occurrence up until then. She didn't even sense him watching her. The drama unfolding on the small screen claimed her full attention.

The hour passed too quickly. When the final credits had faded she said, "That was wonderful, Hunter. I've never been so moved by a television show. Maybe because the people and their problems were so real."

"That's what I've been trying to get across to the network chiefs, but they don't think there's an audience for quality shows. They're convinced that all the viewers want are sitcoms, games shows and dramas full of sex and violence. Those are what pull in the numbers."

"Why not, if that's all there is on?"

He smiled wryly. "Would you like to take a shot at convincing Dennison of that? You're prettier than I am."

Max came in with a plate of hors d'oeuvres, announcing, "It's cocktail time. What can I fix you?"

"Is it that late?" Bliss got up reluctantly. "I'd better be going."

"And leave me stuck with an extra lobster? Do you know what those things cost?" Max demanded. "I thought you were staying for dinner so I went out and shopped."

"You shouldn't have done that," she objected.

"*Now* you tell me!"

"I never said I was staying," she said helplessly. "I only came over to talk to Hunter."

"Well, you're through now. Do you have another date?"

Bliss sent Hunter a silent plea for help. He probably had plans for the evening, and she was reluctant to admit she didn't. He was no help, though. He seemed as interested as Max in her reply.

They were both looking at her expectantly, so she was forced to say, "Well, no, I don't have a date, but I'm sure Hunter does."

"He hasn't had a date since you left," Max answered. "You'd be doing him a favor. I think the boss has lost his touch."

Instead of reacting as he usually did, Hunter merely chuckled. "You'd better give in gracefully. Max can present more arguments than you can find excuses for."

"He's putting you on the spot," she murmured.

"If that's your only reason, don't give it another thought. I didn't have any plans for tonight."

"See, what did I tell you?" Max crowed. "He's a pitiful case."

Hunter arched a sardonic eyebrow at him. "Overkill isn't necessary. She accepted."

The atmosphere changed subtly when Max left them alone. It did for Bliss, at any rate. She'd had a valid reason for being there before, now the occasion was purely social. But things had changed between them. They couldn't go back to being casual friends, at least she couldn't.

Hunter wasn't having the same trouble. No tension was evident in his lithe body as he went behind the bar and filled the ice bucket. He was the perfect host, but nothing in his manner indicated this evening was special.

"What would you like?" he asked pleasantly.

"Whatever you're having, only much milder." She turned her attention to the plate of hors d'oeuvres on the coffee table. "Oh, good. Max made those little cheese things I love."

"He likes you."

"How can you tell? Most of his remarks are critical."

"That's the tip-off. He's only polite to people he doesn't care about."

Bliss laughed. "He must be crazy about *you*."

"We manage to get along without inflicting serious damage on each other," Hunter observed dryly.

"Come on, admit it. You're fond of him, too."

He smiled. "I suppose so, but don't breathe a word of it to Max. He'd be even more impossible to live with. My life isn't my own now."

"You're his family. Although I can't figure out if he considers you a brother or a son," Bliss joked. "Doesn't he have any family of his own?"

"None that he's ever mentioned. Max came to work for me ten years ago, and I don't know any more about his prior life now than I did then."

"You're so close, it's strange that he never told you anything about himself. Aren't you curious?"

"Naturally, but I respect his privacy. Even though he doesn't respect mine," Hunter added, laughing. "The man has absolutely no scruples. He also insists on having everything his way."

"I'm finding that out," she answered ruefully. "I can't believe I'm staying for dinner. I was furious when I came in."

"Do you feel better about things now?" Hunter asked gravely.

"I suppose so. I only wish . . ."

"I know. That you'd never gotten involved with any of us in the first place."

How could she wish that? Happiness was being with Hunter again. He'd made her realize she'd been sleep-walking through life. Maybe waking up involved pain, but moments like this were worth it.

His breath caught as some of Bliss's emotions showed on her expressive face. He moved toward her as though drawn by a magnet. They were gazing into each other's eyes as Max came to announce dinner was ready.

"Boy, is my timing lousy," he muttered to himself.

Bliss privately agreed with him. The old magic had been starting to build between Hunter and herself. Or was that just wishful thinking? No evidence remained in Hunter's manner.

"It's about time," he remarked to Max. "Bliss and I thought dinner was only an idle rumor."

"You want it fast, or you want it good?" Max demanded. "Sit down and start eating."

Instead of setting the large dining room table, he had placed a small table by the window. Candlelight cast a soft glow over heavy silver flatware and thin china. Adding to the ambience was the lovely view through the wide glass window. Floodlights on the lawn illuminated colorful beds of flowers.

"What a beautiful setting, Max," Bliss exclaimed. "It's like something out of a magazine."

"I thought this would be cozier than shouting at each other from opposite ends of the big table," he replied.

"Much cozier," Hunter remarked, gazing impassively at him.

Max returned his look with one of innocence before departing for the kitchen.

"This is such a lovely house," Bliss remarked.

"It's comparatively modest by Hollywood standards. You should see Dennison's place. He has a small theater complete with a projection booth, also a billiard room, sauna and every other toy coveted by man or woman."

"Is he married?"

"For the fourth time."

"How could anyone marry four times?" Bliss exclaimed.

Hunter smiled sardonically. "It's an activity reserved for the rich. You have to be able to afford heavy alimony."

"What a horrible thing to say!"

"But true, unfortunately. Divorce lawyers include their business cards with the wedding gift."

"Doesn't anyone in this town believe in love?"

"Obviously the happy couples do. That's why they get married so often."

"I don't know why they bother."

"My sentiments exactly."

Bliss looked at his handsome, jaded face with a feeling of hopelessness. Although she knew the answer already she asked, "You don't believe in true love? The kind that lasts."

"I believe the people involved *think* it will last. I'm not as cynical as I sound. But our business has built-in pitfalls. For one thing, the people are very glamorous, both men and women. They face temptation every day they go to work."

"People in ordinary jobs face temptation, too," she argued. "But if they're really in love, they don't jeopardize a meaningful relationship."

"Talk to me after you've been here a while and fallen in and out of love a few times."

"When I fall in love it will be forever." Bliss felt like crying as she realized that was true.

"I hope it happens that way for you," he said gently.

She summoned up a semblance of a smile. "That's a rotten thing to say since you're convinced he'll leave me."

Hunter didn't try to match her joking tone. His eyes were bleak as he answered, "Or you'll leave him."

"Don't you know of *any* happy marriages?" she asked wistfully.

"There are some," he admitted. "Two of my good friends have been married for fifteen years. It's quite a feat because Carole is with a ballet troupe that travels all over the world, and Mark is a film cutter here in Hollywood."

"That sounds like Roger's story, only his marriage didn't survive the separations. He's pretty cut up over the divorce. She was the one who wanted it."

"Did you like Roger? Aside from the misunderstanding."

"Yes, he's very easy to talk to. We got along really well together."

"I thought you would."

"You know me better than I know myself," she commented lightly.

He gave her a forced smile. "It's a gift I have when it comes to other people. I'm only mixed up about my own emotions."

"I think you're in complete control of your life, but I hope I never become as disillusioned as you are," she answered quietly.

"I've done everything wrong with you, haven't I, Bliss?" he asked heavily.

She stared down at her plate. "No, you've shown me nothing but kindness. I'm the misfit. You must be terribly tired of my criticizing your way of life."

He covered her hand tightly. "Believe it or not, we share the same values."

It was too bad they didn't share the same feelings, also. She managed a smile. "Then there's hope for both of us. Maybe we'll each find true love and live happily ever after."

"I sincerely hope so." After a quivering moment he removed his hand and changed the subject. "I raised hell at the studio today. You should be getting a check soon."

"That's good news. I've been charging like a cavalry company."

"It's the American way. I wouldn't be surprised if future generations have to look up the word cash in the dictionary."

The rest of the meal was accompanied by light banter with no undercurrents. Neither wanted to venture out again into the deep water that held hidden shoals.

Max served dinner leisurely, with a surprising lack of comment. He presented and removed courses with the silence and expertise of a well-trained waiter, neither interrupting nor intruding on their conversation. His restraint vanished when he placed a hazelnut torte and a silver pot of coffee in the middle of the table.

"You can serve yourselves dessert. I have to leave."

Hunter looked at him blankly. "Why?"

"I just heard a friend of mine took sick. I have to go see him."

"That excuse about sitting up with a sick friend went out with burlesque. We aren't married, Max. If you want to play poker, just say so."

"Okay, I want to play poker. Leave the dishes. I'll clean up in the morning." As he left the room, Max said over his shoulder, "Don't expect me back. This might be an all-night game."

"That was certainly sudden," Bliss commented.

Hunter's eyes glinted angrily. "We're going to have a serious talk when he gets back."

"We're almost finished with dinner, anyway. Does it really matter that he took off?"

"I'm sick and tired of having Max meddle in my affairs," he said through gritted teeth.

"I don't understand. What does his poker game have to do with you?"

"You believed that excuse?"

"Of course. Why wouldn't I? Where do *you* think he went?"

Hunter's expression softened as he gazed at her bewildered face. "You're right, I'm overreacting. Let's have our coffee."

"Not until you tell me what's going on. Why would you care that Max went off and left us? It isn't as though I can't pour—"

She stopped as comprehension dawned. Hunter didn't want to be alone with her. As long as Max could be counted on to pop in on them every few minutes, she couldn't expect Hunter to get romantic. Bliss was stiff with outrage. Did he think she was just waiting to fling herself into his arms? She'd correct *that* misconception immediately!

"I'll clear the table and then I have to leave, too," she said, rising.

"We haven't had dessert yet."

"I couldn't eat another morsel."

"At least have a cup of coffee," he suggested.

"Coffee keeps me awake."

"You don't have to rush off, Bliss," he said quietly. "I won't take advantage of the situation."

His chivalry didn't impress her. They both knew that wasn't what was bothering him. But if he wanted to play it that way, she could, too.

"I'm sure you'd be a perfect gentleman, but I'm anxious to get home. It's been a long day."

"I hope tomorrow will go smoother."

"Actually I enjoyed my session with Roger before our misunderstanding. He's very sympathetic. I think we'll get along famously now that everything is clear to me." She picked up the untouched torte. "I'll take this in the kitchen and be on my way."

"Just leave everything. I'll take care of it."

"Well, if you don't mind," she agreed promptly.

Hunter followed her out to her car, looking as though he wanted to say something and was having trouble phrasing it. Since Bliss didn't want to hear any more insincere excuses, she didn't give him a chance to get a word out.

"It's been a very productive evening. I'm glad we resolved our differences. If any future problems arise, Roger can take care of them from now on."

"Bliss, I didn't mean to—"

"It makes a lot more sense than running to you constantly. Not that I anticipate any further trouble. We should be able to finish the script in record time. Then we can all get back to doing what we really want to do," she couldn't help adding with a touch of bitterness.

"Have you given any thought to what you'll do afterward?" Hunter asked when she finally paused for breath.

"I have all kinds of plans," she lied.

"Like what?" He frowned. "You'd better discuss any deals with me before you accept them."

"That won't be necessary. I'm not the babe in the woods I was when I first arrived."

"You've learned about the world's wicked ways in one week on your own?" he asked ironically.

"I took a crash course," she answered tersely, opening the car door. "Thanks for dinner."

"It was an unexpected pleasure," he replied politely, although his moody expression didn't indicate as much.

Bliss hadn't noticed before that the light over her front door was burned out. When her key eluded her in the depths of her large handbag she uttered a sound of annoyance.

"Having trouble?" a male voice asked.

A man was looming over her in the darkness. "You startled me." She gasped.

"Sorry about that. I assumed you heard me coming." His interest quickened as he got a better look at her lovely face. "The last thing I'd want to do is startle a beautiful girl." When Bliss rummaged for her key without responding, he said, "You're new around here, aren't you?"

"Yes," she answered, hoping he'd take a hint from her curt tone.

He didn't. His voice deepened as he said, "The neighborhood is definitely improving."

Bliss's fingers finally closed around her key, but she was reluctant to open the door with him standing so close.

A more comprehensive look wasn't reassuring. He was quite tall and appeared to be in excellent condition. A tight black turtleneck sweater showed off a broad chest and muscular shoulders as he leaned his weight against one upraised arm braced against the door frame.

The moonlight on his face showed conventional, although rather vapid, good looks. Regular features were capped by faultlessly styled blond hair. He resembled a lot of the men Bliss had glimpsed around the studio, but some indefinable quality about him turned her off.

She returned his gaze coolly. "Don't let me keep you from wherever you were going."

"My plans are flexible." He smiled confidently.

Before she could reply, a rectangle of light streamed onto the central patio and Shelley came running out of her apartment. "Kirk, wait! You forgot your—" The landlady's words stopped abruptly as she noticed Bliss beside the man.

"You didn't tell me you had a new tenant," he remarked.

"I didn't tell you the washing machine broke down, either."

Shelley's acid tone didn't deter him. "Aren't you going to introduce us?"

"Bliss Goodwin, Kirk Talbot," she said grudgingly.

"Not *the* Bliss Goodwin," he exclaimed.

Shelley's displeasure deepened at the added interest in his eyes. "What are the odds against two women having a name like that?"

He ignored her, gazing at Bliss with excitement. "Who would ever expect to find *you* in a place like this?"

"Well, thanks a lot!" Shelley said.

"You know what I mean, sugarbabe. She's the hottest thing around right now." Kirk turned back to Bliss. "Have they started casting your docudrama yet?"

"I really wouldn't know," Bliss murmured.

If her landlady was serious about this man, she had big problems. Bliss had a feeling he strayed often. Shelley certainly had nothing to fear from her, but it was a no-win situation. How did you tell a woman you thought her boyfriend was a creep?

"Why don't we all go somewhere and have a drink?" Kirk suggested.

"No thanks," Bliss declined. "I have to work tomorrow."

"Nobody goes to bed this early. Just one quick drink," he coaxed.

"She said no," Shelley told him sharply.

"Who asked you?" Kirk's expression turned ugly. "Don't you realize she's doing a Hunter Lord production? She might even know him personally."

"Which one of them do *you* want to get personal with?" Shelley asked scathingly.

"Oh, for God's sake! When are you going to stop being so damn suspicious?" he demanded.

"When I find a leash your size."

"That would deprive you of all the fun of spying on me," he answered mockingly.

Bliss was becoming increasingly embarrassed as their argument turned nasty, although they seemed oblivious of her presence. Finally she couldn't take any more.

"Uh...good night. It was nice meeting you." She immediately felt like an idiot for the inane pleasantry.

Kirk turned back to her swiftly. "Are you sure you won't change your mind?"

"I really can't." She unlocked the door and slipped inside with one fluid movement.

"I'm surprised you didn't make a date with her right in front of me." Shelley's furious voice carried through the door.

"Don't be a jerk. All I wanted to do was talk about her movie. She might have been able to get me a part in it, but you fixed that, barging in and acting like a shrew."

"I came to tell you I picked up your cleaning today," Shelley replied icily. "I also paid the C.O.D. charges on your new sport coat and slacks."

"They came?" Kirk's sulkiness turned to pleasure. "That was quick. I only ordered them last week."

"You'll have to pay for these yourself," she warned.

"Sure, baby, as soon as I get my unemployment check."

Their voices trailed off as they walked away, their quarrel diminishing for the moment at least.

Bliss was getting ready for bed when the doorbell rang. Now what? she wondered. Would this day never end? Putting on a bathrobe she went to the door.

Shelley stood outside, her expression ominous. "I want to talk to you." She came inside without being asked.

Bliss sighed. "Can't it wait until tomorrow?"

"No, it can't. I want you to stay away from Kirk," Shelley ordered. "He's mine."

"Congratulations." Bliss was reaching the end of her patience. "I assure you I have no designs on him."

"Don't hand me that! I've seen the effect Kirk has on women."

Nausea was the first one that occurred to Bliss, but she didn't mention it. "Aren't you overreacting? I was getting out my key, and he merely stopped to say hello in passing."

"You weren't exactly discouraging him."

"I was looking for my key, for heaven's sake!"

"You can make up any story you want, I've heard them all. I just want to warn you. Keep your hands off him, or I'll make you sorry you ever moved in here."

"I'm beginning to regret it already," Bliss replied tautly.

"That's fine with me. I'll tear up your lease and you can move out tomorrow." Before Bliss could answer, Shelley stormed out, banging the door behind her.

Bliss was trembling after the ugly scene. Where would she find another apartment this reasonable? She was just getting settled and starting to feel at home, after a week of living without a phone and waiting for people to come and connect things. Did she have to go through all of that again?

Bliss squared her shoulders. No way! It was time she stopped letting people push her around. Whether Shelley liked it or not, she was staying. It wouldn't be easy, but nothing had been. She could handle it.

Roger was delighted to see her the next morning. "I'm so glad you came back. I felt terrible about what happened yesterday."

"I was sorry, too, after Hunter told me it wasn't your fault."

"Is everything all right now?" he asked hesitantly. "I typed up a rough draft using the material you gave me yesterday. Will it be all right to use it?"

"I'd like to see it first," she answered prudently.

"Of course. Hunter made that clear from the beginning."

While Bliss read the typewritten pages, Roger brought her coffee, then went to sit behind his desk. Finally she looked up with shining eyes.

"This is wonderful, Roger! You've captured them marvelously. Some of these things are exactly what Dad would say."

He looked gratified. "That's high praise. I tried, of course, but I wasn't sure I'd succeeded."

"Oh, you did! The part where they explained to me where we were going and why was very touching. That's just the way it happened."

"It's completely accurate, then?"

"Except for a few things, like how they disposed of their property. Dad turned everything into cash. He was a lot shrewder than you portrayed him."

"I just naturally assumed...I mean, Hunter indicated you didn't inherit anything."

"The money went for medical supplies through the years, plus various other things like farming equipment. Then there were my college expenses and school supplies for the village children. I'd like you to show how caring these two people were."

They discussed revisions until noon, when Roger suggested lunch. "I should have made reservations somewhere. We'll have to wait for a table at any decent restaurant, but we can have a drink while we're waiting."

"That will take so long. How about one of those fast-food places?"

He made a face. "The commissary here is preferable."

"That's an even better idea. Let's eat here. It will save time."

"You're going to give the rest of us a bad name," he teased. "People in our business are used to taking long, expensive lunches."

"I'll order the highest priced thing on the menu," she promised.

The commissary reminded Bliss of her college days. The large room was unprepossessing, and the noise level was high. Laughing groups of casually dressed people talked together and traded jokes with friends at other tables.

Bliss was enjoying the relaxed atmosphere—until Hunter appeared with Mona Jensen. Their entry caught everyone's attention, including Roger's. When he waved, they came over to say hello.

"Care to join us?" Roger asked.

Hunter hesitated, but Mona said, "We'd love to."

"I didn't expect to see you in the low-rent district," Roger joked to Hunter.

"I was furious at him for not taking me someplace glamorous, but this really turned into a stroke of luck," Mona said. "I've been wanting to get together with you," she told Bliss. "I need to start studying your mannerisms."

"I don't know if I have any," Bliss answered.

"Everyone does." Mona stared at her appraisingly. "Is that the way you wore your hair on the island?"

"No, it was longer, and I wore it in a braid."

Mona fingered her own long silky hair. "That could be very effective twined with gardenias. Or maybe orchids might be more exotic."

"Neither one grew on the island, and if they had I wouldn't have bothered," Bliss replied evenly.

"What else did you have to do all day?" She gazed at Bliss with awe. "I really admire you. I'd have gone bananas without even the bare necessities."

"Like makeup." Hunter smiled indulgently. "Mona has been known to have an anxiety attack when she leaves her lipstick at home."

"That's not true." She pouted. "You've seen me without makeup lots of times."

From the intimate look that passed between them, Bliss got the impression that Hunter had seen her in a lot less. Were they relighting old flames? Or hadn't the flames ever died?

Mona turned her attention back to Bliss. "I'd like to spend a whole day with you. When will you have some free time?"

"That's hard to say," Bliss answered evasively. "I'm working with Roger every day."

"How about the weekend?" Mona's face lit up. "Why don't we all get together at Hunter's house? He can give us lunch around the pool, and you can show me what to do with my hair when it gets wet. There will be a lot of scenes in the ocean, and I don't want to come out of the water looking a total mess."

"That's the way *I* looked," Bliss said bluntly.

"I'll bet you didn't." Roger's eyes wandered appreciatively over her classic features. "I can picture you as Neptune's daughter, with a garland of coral for a crown."

"You have a writer's imagination." Bliss smiled.

"I hope so, but in your case I don't have to use it."

"Where's the waiter?" Hunter asked abruptly. "The service in this place gets worse every day."

A waiter hurried over when Hunter caught his attention, and for a few minutes they all concentrated on their orders. Mona was only temporarily distracted, however.

When the waiter left she said, "How about Sunday, Hunter? Is it a date?"

"I don't know if I was included, but I'm available," Roger remarked.

"The more the merrier," Mona said. "You are free on Sunday, Bliss?"

She couldn't think of a single excuse on the spur of the moment. "Maybe Hunter isn't," she answered weakly.

"If he isn't, we'll use his pool, anyway," Mona said serenely. "I know where to find everything."

"I hope you can make it," Roger told Hunter with a grin. "It sounds like a great party."

Bliss met Hunter's eyes briefly, encountering the same reluctance. He didn't want to spend the day with her, either—but for a different reason. The bite of hamburger she forced down tasted like sawdust.

Chapter Six

Bliss's spirits were flagging when she arrived home that afternoon, and catching sight of Shelley on the patio didn't improve them any. Since she didn't feel up to another encounter at that moment, she ignored the other woman.

"Bliss, wait," Shelley called. "Can I talk to you for a minute?"

"No," she replied firmly, unlocking her door. "We have nothing to discuss. I'm not moving."

"I'm glad to hear it." Shelley walked over to her.

"What?" Bliss paused in astonishment.

"I want to apologize for acting like such a jerk last night."

"Oh . . . well . . . that's all right."

"No, it isn't." Shelley sighed. "May I come in? I'd rather not have the whole building know my business."

"I guess so." When they were inside, Bliss asked out of innate courtesy, "Would you like some coffee or tea?"

"You don't have anything stronger, do you?"

"I'm sorry, I don't."

"Okay, coffee it is, then." Shelley followed her to the kitchen.

Bliss was wary as she filled the coffeepot and got out cups and saucers. Shelley's changed attitude was welcome, but she was learning not to be too trusting.

Shelley sensed her reserve. "You're being a good sport about this. I wouldn't blame you if you told me to get lost."

"That wouldn't accomplish anything. I'd rather forget the whole incident."

"I'd really like to explain," Shelley insisted. "I knew you weren't making a play for Kirk, that it was the other way around."

"Oh, no, honestly! He was just being friendly."

"Don't bother trying to spare my feelings. Kirk comes on to every attractive woman he runs across. It's a reflex action, the way a knee jerks when you tap it in the right place."

"It can't mean anything, then," Bliss said tentatively.

"It does to me. I'm crazy about the guy," Shelley said morosely. "I ought to throw him out on his ear, but he knows I won't do it."

Bliss couldn't think of anything to say, yet she felt some comment was indicated. "At least you don't have anything to worry about from me."

"I realized that after I calmed down. Women are usually anxious to catch what Kirk is pitching, but you have your own trouble with Hunter Lord. We really picked a couple of winners, didn't we?''

"I'm sorry you got the impression that Hunter and I are...involved,'' Bliss answered carefully. "Nothing could be farther from the truth. As a matter of fact, he's seeing Mona Jensen.''

"I thought that was all over with. The gossip columns have been pairing her with the TV actor, Cullen Wainwright.''

"You can't believe everything you read in the papers.'' Bliss smiled sardonically. "I'm living proof of that.''

"How much of what they printed about you is true?'' Shelley asked curiously.

"I hope you'll see the real story when the documentary is aired. Hunter is trying to be truthful, I'll give him that much, but Mona is one of the problems. She wants to look like Sheena, queen of the jungle, and I'm afraid he isn't used to saying no to her.''

"There's a lot of temperament in this business. A producer has a tough job keeping everyone happy.''

"Mona has an unfair advantage,'' Bliss said angrily. "Whose side do you think he's going to take?''

"Well, it could be worse. At least she'll make you look glamorous.''

"I suppose so.'' Bliss didn't want to talk about Hunter and Mona any longer. "Would you like more coffee?''

"No thanks, I have to go to work.'' Shelley stood. "It's great therapy. I work out all my frustrations through exercise.''

"I should join your class as soon as I can afford it. I let *my* frustrations build up,'' Bliss remarked ruefully.

"Most people do. Why don't you come with me tonight? I'll give you a sample lesson on the house."

"I wasn't hinting," Bliss protested.

"I know you weren't, but I owe you one, anyway. How about it? We'll get something to eat afterward."

Bliss had nothing else to do that night, and it was better than sitting home alone. "Okay, but I don't know much about dancing."

"You will after I get through with you."

Bliss was impressed with the size of Shelley's studio. It was filled with people working out on various types of equipment while loud music blared in the background. The jazzercize classes consisted mostly of women, with a few men sprinkled in.

Shelley's class was well attended, and Bliss soon understood why. She was a very talented dancer. Anyone trying to emulate her movements soon discovered that.

Bliss was grateful when Shelley finally called a break. "I thought I was in good condition, but that woman is awesome," she remarked to the man next to her.

"She's something else all right." He wiped his damp forehead. "Is this your first time here?"

"Yes, but I'll be back."

"This aerobics thing really grows on you," he remarked, glancing over to the corner where Shelley was talking to one of her instructors.

Bliss had a sudden feeling that he was as interested in Shelley as he was in her class. A closer look revealed a pleasant young man with intelligent brown eyes and a friendly, open manner. He didn't have Kirk's theatrical good looks, but he was tall and well built, and in Bliss's opinion, a lot more appealing.

Shelley walked back to the middle of the room, graceful in her black leotard. "All right, rest period is over," she announced. "This time let's really get our heart rate going."

After class was over she said to Bliss, "Well, how did you like it?"

"I used muscles I didn't know I had."

"That's the whole idea."

"I'll try to remember that when I have trouble getting out of bed tomorrow." Bliss laughed. "You're really fantastic. I can't see why you gave up a dancing career."

"I meet a better class of people here," Shelley answered dryly.

"I saw one of them. An awfully nice fellow with curly brown hair. Handsome, too," Bliss added casually.

"That must be David Manning, but I wouldn't exactly call him handsome."

"I like those craggy kind of features on a man."

Shelley looked at her speculatively. "He's your type, a thoroughly nice guy."

If she knew that, why didn't she snap him up? Bliss hid her impatience. "I think he's more interested in you."

"This one you can have with my blessing." Shelley laughed. "You won't be poaching on my territory. David," she called, "come over here. I'd like you to meet Bliss. She's new in town."

"We got acquainted during that torture session you call a class." He smiled.

"You know you love it," she answered. "You wouldn't show up so faithfully otherwise."

"I only come to see you. I keep hoping one of these times you'll go out with me. Is tonight the night?" His tone was joking, but Bliss knew he was serious, even though Shelley didn't seem to realize it.

"I have some things to do, but Bliss isn't busy," she said.

"You're putting the poor man on the spot," Bliss protested. "Besides, we planned to go out for something to eat. I'll wait till you're through with whatever you have to do."

"Why don't I take both of you to dinner?" David offered.

"That would be lovely," Bliss accepted quickly before Shelley had a chance to decline.

Shelley was reluctant at first, but she soon got over her annoyance. David was very good company, and he kept them laughing at his experiences.

"I never knew the advertising business could be so amusing," Shelley commented. "Did someone honestly substitute a porno film for your presentation to a baby food company?"

"It didn't seem funny at the time, but it was only a joke. I explained what happened and salvaged the account."

"You're too nice for your own good," Shelley scolded.

"I gather that isn't a compliment," he said wryly. "Why is it women prefer men who are mean and rotten?"

"They don't if they have any sense," Bliss said.

Shelley raised one eyebrow. "You're a fine one to talk."

"I have a feeling I'm being left out of this conversation," David complained.

"That's what happens when two women get together." Bliss stood. "You two carry on. I have to make notes for my meeting tomorrow." Before Shelley could object, she left them alone.

Hunter put off telling Max about the swimming party until Saturday. Even then he didn't actually tell him, knowing Max would have a few pungent observations.

"Will you make some sandwiches before you leave Sunday morning?" he asked casually.

"It's my day off," Max said indignantly. "Why can't you ever date a bimbo who can cook?"

"I have never dated a bimbo," Hunter stated with dignity.

"Oh, no? How about Taffy Wellbuilt?"

Hunter gave him a frown of annoyance. "Her name was Welby."

"Whatever. Anyway, remember the night you had the party for the big shots you were trying to attract as investors? When one of them said he wanted to see the figures first, she started to take off her clothes."

Hunter smiled reluctantly. "Taffy just happened to be more literal than literate."

"She also had a hell of a body," Max said reminiscently. "If she's your action tomorrow you won't need sandwiches, you'll need oxygen."

"I appreciate your concern, but I'm not seeing Taffy. I'm having a business meeting here."

"Monkey business?"

"Just forget the whole thing. I'll call the deli."

"No need to fly off the handle. I'll make lunch. How many people are you expecting?"

"There will be four of us."

"Men or women?"

Hunter arched a dark eyebrow. "I didn't know menus were male or female."

"Okay, if you don't want to tell me. I realize I'm just a servant around here. Go care about somebody," Max muttered.

"You're the wrong sex to play Lady Macbeth," Hunter observed dryly. "If you must know, I'm having Mona Jensen, Roger Paradine and Bliss. We're going to work on the show."

Max stared at him with a speculative expression, but all he said was, "Should be an interesting afternoon."

Bliss wasn't looking forward to watching Hunter and Mona together, but having Roger there would make it more bearable. His frequent compliments were flattering, especially in front of Hunter. She accepted gladly when Roger suggested picking her up that Sunday.

Mona was already there when they arrived, prompting Bliss to wonder if she'd spent the night. What difference did it make if it was last night or some other one? she thought drearily.

"Where have you two been?" Mona greeted them. "We're starving, but Max wouldn't even give up a nibble until you arrived."

"Isn't this Max's day off?" Bliss asked.

He came up in back of her carrying a tray of drinks. "The boss ordered me to stay and make lunch."

"We could have managed by ourselves," she protested. "That isn't fair."

"It isn't accurate, either," Hunter said. "Max is the fiction writer of the culinary set."

"Do you deny asking me to make sandwiches?"

"That's a little closer to the truth. May we have them now?"

Max had prepared more than sandwiches. The buffet he set out held platters and bowls of delicacies. They feasted on chicken salad, fresh fruit, muffins and flaky croissants. For dessert he'd baked a chocolate cheese-cake that was meltingly delicious.

"Max, this is absolutely divine." Mona closed her eyes in reverence. "Is there any way I can entice you away from Hunter?"

"I couldn't leave the boss. He'd live on potato chips and forget to pick up his shirts at the laundry."

"No wonder he never got married," Roger joked. "Even wives don't perform those services anymore."

Mona gave Hunter a seductive look. "They might if the fringe benefits were attractive enough."

Bliss stood abruptly. "It's getting really hot. I think I'll go for a swim."

"Good idea," Roger said. "I'll join you."

Bliss changed into her bathing suit, trying to forget the intimate look that passed between Hunter and Mona. It only verified what was already self-evident.

She walked quickly out to the pool and dove off the deep end without looking at either of the two.

Roger joined her and they swam together for a while, but he tired before she did. He sat on the steps, watching while she did a surface dive and glided along the bottom of the pool.

"Fantastic!" he said admiringly when she came up for air. "She looks like a mermaid, doesn't she, Hunter?"

"I've remarked on the resemblance myself." Hunter's voice was uninflected, but something flickered in the depths of his eyes.

Bliss's cheeks flamed as she remembered the circumstances. How could he be cruel enough to remind her? Especially with Mona sitting next to him, an example of what he desired in a woman.

"I hope you don't expect me to swim like that," Mona commented. "How would you like to be my double, Bliss?"

"That isn't a bad idea," Roger remarked thoughtfully. "What do you think, Hunter?"

"Bliss might not care to go on location with us."

"I can understand why you wouldn't want to go back there," Mona said sympathetically.

"Of course. It was thoughtless of me," Roger apologized.

"It's not that big a deal." Bliss got out of the pool and picked up a towel. "The circumstances would make a difference. This time I'd have lots of company."

"What was it like?" Mona leaned forward intently. "Did you live right out in the open, or did you find a cave?"

"No, it was only a small atoll. I was lucky there were trees."

"You slept under a tree?" Mona asked incredulously.

"It wasn't that bad. You'll see the hut I built if a storm hasn't flattened it."

"How did you manage to build a hut without tools?" Roger looked at her in awe. "I don't think I could do it *with* them, even power tools."

"You city slickers think 'let there be light' meant electricity," she teased. "Fortunately I learned how the natives build shelters in the villages."

"You still must have needed a hammer and nails, a saw, all sorts of equipment you didn't have," Roger insisted.

"You'd be surprised what you can do if you have to," Bliss answered.

She explained how she'd woven palm fronds for a roof suspended over saplings. Fallen branches, trimmed and lashed together with additional fronds, formed walls. When they were attached to the roof, each supported the other.

"All this took a lot of time, and I could only work during the daylight hours," she said. "There was so much to do that the first couple of months went by fast."

"When the months stretched on, did you ever give up hope of being rescued?" Mona asked soberly.

"Not really, although I got depressed now and then. I might have been more discouraged if I'd known how long I was there, but I didn't try to keep track of time. I simply did what had to be done each day."

"What was there to do after your shelter was built?" Roger asked.

"More things than you can imagine. Every morning I went down to the beach to gather driftwood and anything else that washed up. You wouldn't believe the junk people throw in the ocean. Bottles and plastic containers came in really handy, but one red-letter day I found a plastic fork."

"I'm just beginning to realize all the things we take for granted," Roger said slowly.

"Try running water," Bliss advised. "I had to make trips back and forth to the stream in the middle of the island to haul water back in bottles and coconut shells."

"Wouldn't it have been easier to build your hut next to it?"

"Much easier, but I was afraid I might miss a passing ship or a plane if one went by."

"Couldn't you have put up some kind of signal flag?" Roger asked.

"I didn't have any bright-colored cloth to make one out of, but I spelled out SOS on the beach with large stones that I died with squid ink."

Hunter hadn't taken part in the questioning. He'd simply listened intently, watching Bliss's face with deepening emotion. His voice was husky when he finally said, "I'm glad you're letting us tell your story. You're a portrait in courage."

"Not really. I was afraid a lot of the time," she admitted, although his compliment pleased her enormously.

"All brave people are," he answered gravely.

His respect was like a warm cloak. Hunter did care about her, even if it wasn't the way she wanted. It was something, though.

"You've made everything so vivid," Roger said. "I wish I could see the place for myself."

"Aren't you going on location with the crew?" Bliss asked.

"I have another commitment as soon as I finish this one," he said regretfully.

"You'll see it when the show is aired," Mona consoled him.

"It won't be the same as seeing everything exactly as Bliss left it."

"I hope all my things aren't scattered," she observed.

"What did you have to leave behind?" Mona asked with a puzzled expression.

Bliss smiled. "My set of abalone shell dishes and a bowl of glass floats from fishing nets. I set quite an elegant table after a hatch cover washed ashore."

Mona nodded approvingly. "I admire your style."

Bliss had gradually changed her mind about Mona during the afternoon. Her sexy appearance and seductive manner were misleading. Underneath that gorgeous exterior was a genuinely nice person. That made her an even more formidable rival—if there had been any contest. How could she hope to compete against a woman like that? Bliss concluded sadly.

It was a surprisingly pleasant day, however, and the hours passed swiftly. The sun was low in the sky when Hunter looked at his watch.

"It's after five," he remarked. "Can I fix anyone a drink?"

"We'd better not start drinking this early," Mona warned. "It's apt to be a long night."

"Not for me," he answered. "I'm going to bed early for once. Right after I work up some production schedules."

"Aren't you forgetting something? Tonight is Maggie Cole's party. You promised her you'd be there."

Hunter groaned. "Is that thing tonight?"

"Yes, and you have to go. She's the most influential columnist in town, and she'd never forgive you if you didn't show."

"Those parties are always so crowded she'd probably never know the difference," he offered half-heartedly.

"Maggie's eyesight is as sharp as her tongue. Maybe we can get away early, though." As Mona stood and reached for the cover-up that matched her brief bikini, the eyes of both men were drawn like a magnet to her exquisite figure.

"No maybe about it," Hunter stated firmly.

"Don't sulk, darling. You'll enjoy yourself tonight, I guarantee it. Pick me up at eight." With an airy wave to the others, she left.

"Since we weren't invited with the big kids, how about a movie and dinner afterward?" Roger asked Bliss.

"I'd love it." Her response held more enthusiasm than she felt. "I guarantee *you'll* enjoy yourself, too," she added deliberately, for Hunter's benefit.

Roger grinned. "Sounds promising."

If she'd hoped for a reaction from Hunter, Bliss was disappointed. He merely remarked, "I wish I were going with you."

She and Roger left a short time later. He dropped her off to shower and change, and went home to do the same.

Shelley was coming toward her as she started up the walk. "Where have you been keeping yourself?" she asked. "I haven't seen you around lately."

"Our hours are different. You're gone by the time I get home."

"I thought maybe you were avoiding me after that little stunt you pulled the other night."

"I don't know what you mean."

"Don't pull that innocent act on me. You know what I'm talking about. First you con me into going out with you and David, and then you duck out and leave me alone with him."

"I had to get up early in the morning. Besides, a lot of women would think I did them a favor. He's very amusing."

"If he's such a big deal, why aren't you staking out a claim?"

"Because he isn't interested in me. I gather David's been trying to get a date with you for months."

"So you arranged it. Quite the little matchmaker, aren't you?"

"You must admit you two hit it off well."

"He's a lot of fun," Shelley admitted grudgingly.

"Then what are you complaining about?"

"David is a thoroughly nice guy. He's more your type than mine."

"What do you have against nice guys?"

"I never knew any," Shelley answered with a slight laugh.

"Then it might be a new experience for you. Who knows? David could change your whole way of thinking."

"About Kirk, I suppose you mean."

"Well, it wouldn't hurt to let him know he has some competition."

"You might be right at that, except it wouldn't be fair to David."

"You aren't committing yourself to anything by going out with him."

"That's true." Shelley looked at Bliss speculatively. "Have you ever considered taking your own advice?"

"Are you suggesting we share him?"

"I was referring to Hunter. He's used to having women drop everything when he whistles. It wouldn't be a bad idea for you to start dating other guys, too. And don't tell me again that he doesn't mean anything to you." Shelley's mouth curved with self-mockery. "I can recognize a fellow sufferer when I see one."

Bliss didn't bother to deny it any longer. In a way, it was a relief to talk about her problem with someone who would understand, although she didn't intend to give Shelley all the gruesome details.

"I'll admit I'm attracted to Hunter," she said carefully. "As you pointed out, a lot of women are, women more beautiful and sophisticated than I could ever hope to be. I'm not foolish enough to think I have a chance with him."

"Don't sell yourself short. You can compete with the best of them."

"With Mona Jensen?"

"That's pretty stiff competition," Shelley admitted. "It isn't a lost cause, however. She might have the inside track, but you're definitely in the running, judging by the way he treated you the day you rented the apartment."

"I wish you were right, but Hunter just feels responsible for me. Everything was so strange when I first got here. People tried to take advantage of me, and he got used to taking care of me. I could be his kid sister."

"All the more reason for showing him you're grown up. If you started seeing other men it might give him the necessary jolt."

"I made a date right in front of him today, and it didn't bother him a bit," Bliss replied dolefully.

"You have to give him time for it to sink in. Who was the guy?"

Bliss explained about Roger. "He'll be here shortly. I'd better get dressed."

"Well, have a good time," Shelley said encouragingly. "And don't even think about Hunter."

"Did you put Kirk out of your mind while you were with David?" Bliss asked hopelessly.

Shelley looked surprised. "You know what? That's exactly what I did."

Bliss felt encouraged about Shelley when they parted, but she didn't think Roger was the answer to her own problem. Hunter was a lot harder act to follow than Kirk. With a sigh, she turned on the shower.

* * *

Contrary to her expectations, Bliss enjoyed the evening with Roger. They saw a funny movie and went to an unpretentious place afterward for dinner.

"I owe you a fancy night on the town," he remarked when they were seated at a slightly wobbly table in a small French restaurant. "This is no way to make an impression. First the commissary, and now this."

"You don't have to impress me. Besides, we aren't dressed to go anyplace fancy, and I didn't want to anyway."

"You're so sweet to say so, but I promise you something grand next time. Have you been to the Chanticleer?" he named a currently popular and very expensive restaurant.

"Yes, Hunter took me there."

"I might have known better than to try to outdo him. He really gets around."

Bliss changed the subject. "When do you think we'll start shooting?"

"Quite soon. The show is cast, and Hunter is hiring the production crew now."

"Will they do the scenes on the island first?"

"No, those will come last. It's a big job to take a whole crew that far. You have no idea of the people and equipment involved."

"Where are they all going to stay? Will they pitch tents on the island?"

Roger laughed. "That bunch of urban cowboys? They think a tent is the paper parasol you get in a drink at Trader Vic's."

"But there isn't anyplace close enough to commute from every day."

"Not to worry. Dennison is pouring big bucks into this show. He's chartering a yacht to lie offshore. Everything is strictly first class. When you come out of your swim in the lagoon, someone will be waiting to hand you a robe."

"Do you think Mona really meant it when she asked me to double for her?"

"I'm sure she did. Mona is as anxious as you are to make a quality film."

"Is that why she suggested the nude swimming scenes?" Bliss asked cynically. "I presume she intends to do those herself. Or at least the camera will be on her when she comes out of the water."

Roger grinned. "You can't really blame her. She has her career to think about, and her figure isn't exactly a liability."

"No, I saw you and Hunter eyeing her," Bliss remarked, trying to keep her voice playful.

"We were eyeing you, too," he answered gallantly.

"You don't have to try to make me feel better. I'm aware of the difference in our measurements. That's one of the things that bothered me when Hunter gave her the part."

"I wouldn't worry if I were you. Mona will look a lot different when she's toned down, and she's a good actress. Hunter wouldn't have okayed her otherwise."

"Are you sure?" Bliss concentrated on rolling breadcrumbs into a tiny ball. "A man who's in love with a woman isn't always objective."

"I don't think that would sway Hunter. His business and personal lives are two separate matters. But who told you they were in love?"

"I heard talk," she answered vaguely.

"They had a thing going some time back, but I thought that was all over with."

"That wasn't the impression I got today," Bliss murmured.

"Then I must have missed something."

"She didn't have any trouble persuading him to take her to that party tonight when he obviously didn't want to go."

"Is that all? Hunter knew he had no choice. Even *he* can't risk offending the press."

Bliss wasn't convinced. "I can't imagine Hunter doing anything he didn't really want to do."

"You don't know this industry very well. We all make compromises when we consider the rewards."

She tried not to think about how Hunter was being rewarded that night, not necessarily for good behavior.

Bliss was hurrying down the hall to Roger's office the next morning when she almost ran into Clay Dennison. The studio chief greeted her warmly.

"How are things going, Bliss? Is everyone taking good care of you?"

"Everything's fine, thanks."

"Splendid. Mona tells me she wants you to double for her in some swimming scenes."

Bliss stared at him in surprise. "How did you know? She only asked me yesterday afternoon."

"I saw her at a party last night. We discussed it, and I told her I thought it was an excellent idea. I'll see that you get on-screen credit."

"That won't be necessary. I really don't care."

He chuckled indulgently. "I can tell you haven't been in Hollywood very long. You wouldn't believe what actresses will do for screen credits."

"But that's just the point. I'm not an actress. I don't need the recognition."

"It will be excellent publicity for the film," he insisted. "People will tune in to see the real you, if for no other reason."

That was when Bliss understood it wasn't altruism on his part. "All right, if you think it's important," she conceded tepidly.

"Trust me. We have to keep the momentum going until airtime, and this is just the ticket. It's time you met the critics, too. I've invited all the top ones to a party at my house on Wednesday night, and I'd like you to be there. The media is very important."

Bliss felt the familiar knot tightening in her stomach at the thought of facing prying eyes and impertinent questions again. She'd thought that was all over with.

"I'll send a car for you at eight," Clay was saying.

"Well, I . . . I don't know if I can make it."

"I don't think you understood me, Bliss. Favorable publicity will guarantee us a large viewing audience. You wouldn't want to disappoint all the people who are working so hard to make the show a success." His voice was silky, but it held an underlying implacability.

"Will the whole cast be there?"

She didn't like to ask about Hunter specifically, but his presence would certainly make things easier. In spite of their ups and downs, she depended on him. He was her security blanket.

"The entire happy family." Dennison was all geniality once more when he sensed her capitulation. "Can we count on you?"

"Yes, I'll be there," she answered with as much enthusiasm as she could muster.

"Splendid. Then it's all settled." With a smile, he continued down the corridor.

Bliss went into Roger's office without seeing Hunter at the end of the hall.

"Does Bliss have a problem?" Hunter asked when Dennison reached him.

"None visible to the naked eye. That girl has really blossomed. Who would believe she's the same little waif who got off the plane looking like a ragpicker's kid just a few weeks ago?"

"She hasn't changed since the last time you saw her. In your office," Hunter reminded him.

"I never notice things like that when I'm talking money." Clay laughed.

"I should have remembered your priorities," Hunter said dryly.

"Don't put on that holier-than-thou act. You squeezed me like a lemon on her contract."

"I merely kept you honest. She's worth every penny."

"I'll have to agree with you there. This latest idea about putting her in the film is money in the bank. If she looks the way I think she does in the buff, the reruns will be a bonanza. Everyone who missed the show the first time around will tune in for a look-see."

"Bliss wouldn't consider doing nude scenes," Hunter said sharply.

"She will if she's approached right. This flick could launch her into show business."

"That isn't what she wants."

"Since when are you that naive? She's no different from any other woman in this town. Give her a taste of stardom, and she'll be scratching and clawing her way to the top like all the rest."

Hunter's jawline was rigid. "I hope you're wrong."

"Wait and see," Clay said confidently. "I'm going to start the ball rolling Wednesday night with a party for the critics. I'll expect you and Mona there, too."

"Did you strong-arm Bliss into accepting?" Hunter demanded.

"Why would you think a thing like that?"

"She avoids the media like a plague. They've given her a bad time since the moment she arrived. You saw that circus at the airport."

"The poor kid was on her own then. Now she has the protection of the network." Dennison's eyes took on a predatory gleam. "She's under my wing, you might say."

"The one that isn't sheltering your wife, I presume." Hunter's expression was sardonic.

"I was speaking metaphorically," Clay answered suavely. "You'll be there Wednesday night, won't you?"

"Count on it," Hunter replied harshly.

Chapter Seven

In spite of her original reluctance, Bliss was filled with anticipation as she got dressed on Wednesday night. Her first Hollywood party was bound to be eventful, and she was looking forward to seeing Clay Dennison's fabled house. The fact that Hunter would be there, too, contributed to the excitement. She hadn't seen him since the Sunday at his home.

The doorbell rang as she was trying to decide what to wear. Carrying a flame-colored chiffon gown, she answered the door in her bathrobe.

Shelley took note of the dress over her arm. "I came to ask if you wanted to go to the studio with me, but it looks like you have better plans. Hot date?"

"No date at all. Mr. Dennison is sending a car for me. He's having a party."

Shelley whistled. "You're really breathing rarefied air." Her gaze suddenly sharpened. "What kind of party?"

"That's the downside. It's to publicize the documentary. All the media will be there."

"That's okay, then. I though maybe it was an intimate party for two."

"Don't be ridiculous! Mr. Dennison is married."

"They're the worst kind. When are you going to wise up?"

"I don't have time for a lecture. Come in and help me decide what to wear."

Shelley looked through Bliss's extensive wardrobe before making her decision. "The one you picked out, definitely. Red will make you stand out like a beacon."

"That wasn't what I had in mind," Bliss answered doubtfully.

"When you've got it, flaunt it, pal." Shelley looked at her appraisingly. "What do you plan to do with your hair?"

"Comb it." Bliss smiled.

"This calls for something special. Sit down."

Shelley picked up a brush and comb from the dressing table and proceeded to create an intricate hairdo. She swept part of Bliss's hair up to her crown and left the rest to float freely, like a flow of golden honey. Little curls pulled out at random made the total effect sexy, yet at the same time artless.

"Wow!" Bliss stared at her reflection. "You're a genius. For the first time, I look as though I belong in Hollywood."

"You'll knock 'em dead," Shelley said with satisfaction.

"I'm starting to get nervous. What do I talk to these people about?"

"That's easy. If it's a man, just say no."

"I'm serious," Bliss protested.

"You think I'm not? Put on your dress and I'll zip you up."

The red chiffon was sleeveless and backless. It was a seductive dress, meant to call attention to the wearer. Bliss's body was provocatively outlined under the soft fabric without being really visible. She wasn't aware of the signals she was sending out since the gown wasn't actually revealing.

Shelley walked out to the car with her when the chauffeur arrived. He waited by the stretch limo while they said goodbye, self-effacing in his black suit and visored cap.

"You've certainly brought class to the neighborhood," Shelley joked. "Have a good time and tell me all about it tomorrow."

Bliss was beset by sudden qualms. "I won't know anybody there. I'd probably have a better time at the studio with you."

"Don't be a chump. It will be an experience. Who knows what could happen tonight?"

Clay Dennison's estate was perched on a mountaintop overlooking Benedict Canyon. The sprawling modern house looked more like a hotel than a residence, especially with its tennis court and swimming pool. An attendant in a white coat opened the door as the chauffeur stopped in the middle of the circular driveway.

A maid took Bliss's wrap in the entry hall and directed her to the living room where a buzz of conversation told her the party was already in progress. She stood hesitantly at the top of the steps to the sunken living room, looking in vain for a familiar face. Bliss didn't see Hunter and Clay at the far end of the large room, but they saw her.

"Ah, here's Bliss," Clay said, his eyes lighting up. "Doesn't she look sensational?"

Hunter's expression was less approving. "I've never seen her gotten up like that. She's usually so natural."

"You pick your type, and I'll pick mine. Excuse me while I greet my guest."

Hunter watched as Dennison made his way through the crowded room. Before he could reach Bliss, she was surrounded by several other men. Hunter could catch only a brief glimpse of her face, but he could see that she was smiling.

If he'd been closer he would have realized it was a set smile. Bliss didn't know how to deal with the brittle, slightly suggestive repartee of the men around her. She breathed a sigh of relief when Clay joined them.

"Have a heart, fellows," he said. "Let the poor girl get inside."

"That's where the competition is," one of the men answered. He turned back to Bliss. "How about giving me an exclusive interview? Let's go someplace where we can be alone."

"Forget God's masterpiece of mediocrity," another man told her. "I'm the one who can do you justice."

"Why don't you talk to Mona Jensen while I get Bliss a drink?" Clay coaxed. "We'll have a little news item for you later." He deftly led Bliss away in spite of their objections.

"I'm glad you came along," she confided. "Reporters always intimidate me."

"They're a necessary evil." He shrugged. "You'll get used to them. What can I get you to drink?"

"Nothing right now, thanks."

"Are you sure?" He sounded surprised. "A little Scotch? A vodka martini?"

Bliss decided she'd probably look conspicuous without a drink in her hand. "Well, maybe I'll have one of those." She indicated a waiter with a silver tray full of crystal flutes.

Clay beckoned the man over and handed her one of the glasses. "I told Hunter you had champagne tastes." His rather thin lips curved in a satisfied smile.

"Is Hunter here? I didn't see him."

"He's around somewhere." When she continued to scan the room, Clay said, "Did you want him for something?"

"No, he's one of the few people I know here, that's all," she replied hastily. "You have a beautiful home, Mr. Dennison."

"Clay, please. Mr. Dennison sounds so unapproachable, and you'll find I'm not that kind of person. Would you like to see the rest of the house?"

"Very much. Could I?"

"I'll give you a guided tour." He took her arm.

"I don't want to take you away from your guests," she protested. "I'll just wander through by myself if you don't mind."

"I wouldn't want you to get lost." He smiled. "Besides, no one here will miss me as long as the liquor holds out."

Bliss set her glass down unobtrusively as Clay led her out of the living room to a wide hallway. Across the hall was a formal dining room dramatically furnished. A plate-glass table was supported by pink marble columns that matched the marble buffet attached to one long, mirrored wall.

All of the many rooms were eye-catching in some way. Clay's office had a stark, black-and-white color scheme, extending even to the paintings on the walls. A den had a circular couch in the middle of the room with a sunken fireplace in the center.

"This is unbelievable," Bliss murmured as he pushed a button that activated electrically operated drapes. They purred open to frame the light of the city in the distance. "What a glorious view you have!"

"I'll show you an even better one." He took her hand and led her through more hallways to a distant wing of the house.

"I understand now why you thought I'd get lost. I've never seen anyplace this huge," she marveled. "You must do a lot of entertaining."

"A certain amount." He slanted a glance to her. "Do you like parties?"

"I must admit I prefer small ones where you can really get to know people."

"My sentiments exactly." He gave her hand a little squeeze. "We're kindred spirits."

They had reached a bedroom suite that looked like something out of a movie. Thick beige carpeting matched the wall color exactly, providing a neutral background for large, vibrant paintings, mostly of nudes. Some of them were highly erotic. After an embarrassed glance, Bliss turned her attention to the oversize bed sitting on a raised platform facing a wall of windows. The headboard of blond wood looked like the instrument panel of an airplane.

"What are all those knobs and dials for?" she asked.

"Anything you like." He moved over to demonstrate. "Television, radio, tape deck. This button turns off the lights, or dims them." The lamps subsided to a muted glow as Clay adjusted them.

"You don't have to get out of bed for anything," Bliss exclaimed.

"Sometimes it's inconvenient," he murmured.

"I suppose one of those gadgets works the drapes like the one in the den. What fun to see what the weather is like before you even get out of bed in the morning."

"I find it more fascinating at night."

As the draperies drew apart, a wonderland of multi-colored lights appeared. The darkness was spangled with a million jewels outlining distant buildings and free-ways.

Bliss was dazzled by the spectacle. "I could look at this for hours."

"That could be arranged," he answered softly, turning the lights lower.

"What are you doing?" she asked sharply.

"Giving you a better view."

Shelley's warning rang belatedly in Bliss's head. She couldn't honestly believe Clay was about to make a pass at her, but the atmosphere was suddenly charged. Perhaps it was the quiet at this end of the house, or the intimacy of being in his bedroom alone with him. That was another thing that made her uneasy. She hadn't seen any feminine articles to indicate his wife shared the suite.

"I've monopolized you long enough," she said lightly. "We'd better get back to the party."

As she started to walk past him to the door, Clay's hands circled her wrists. "You're not afraid of me, are you, my dear?"

"No, of course not."

"That's good, because I want to be your friend." His voice was silky. "I have big plans for you."

"You're very kind, but if you mean a career in show business, I'm really not interested."

"Don't be hasty, Bliss. The rewards can be great," he said persuasively. "You're a girl who likes nice things, I can tell."

"Even if I were interested, it wouldn't work out. I don't have any talent."

"You're too modest, but I find that refreshing."

"We really should be getting back to the party," she said hesitantly.

"You're right. We'll discuss this another time. How about—"

He paused as the lights were suddenly turned on full. A stunning woman stood in the doorway regarding them impassively. She had flaming red hair and a gorgeous figure.

"I thought this was where I'd find you," she said.

"Giselle, my love, I'd like you to meet Bliss Goodwin," Clay answered smoothly. "She wanted to see the house."

"The tour always stops here, doesn't it? I'm Clay's wife, incidentally," she told Bliss. "A fact he often forgets to mention."

"I'm very happy to meet you," Bliss responded uncomfortably. "You have a beautiful home."

"That's what all of Clay's little friends say. But you should try chatting in the living room sometime. That's where we usually entertain."

He shot his wife a look of annoyance. "We were just on our way there. Will you join us, or would you prefer to phone Don Rickles for more material?"

Bliss was repelled by their biting remarks to each other, and appalled that she was the cause of them—this time. She could tell their sparring matches were a fairly common occurrence.

"Excuse me," she mumbled. "I have to speak to someone."

Hunter was the first person Bliss saw when she reentered the living room. Her pleasure was tempered somewhat by the scowl on his face.

"Where the hell have you been?" he demanded roughly.

"Clay was showing me the house."

"How kind of him." He sneered.

"*I* thought so."

Bliss's temper was starting to simmer. After the nasty scene between the Dennisons, she didn't need another one with Hunter. What was he so grouchy about, anyway?

"It didn't seem strange to you that he left a houseful of guests to give you a private tour?" Hunter asked.

"I assumed everyone else had already seen it," she answered coolly.

He swore under his breath. "When are you going to get some sense? Do I have to watch you every minute?"

Her anger was joined by misery. Hunter was making it abundantly clear that she was a millstone around his neck. Well, she could do something about *that*, at least.

"Nobody appointed you my guardian." She lifted her chin and glared at him. "I neither need nor desire anything further from you."

"Then God help you, because nobody else will. You don't even have the sense to know when a man is coming on to you."

"If you're referring to Clay, of course I knew it."

Hunter was slightly taken aback. "And that didn't bother you?"

"Why should it? He's a very influential man. He could do a lot for my career."

"What career?" Hunter asked bluntly.

"The one Clay could open up for me. He told me so himself."

Hunter stared at her incredulously. "I can't believe this. All it took was one party?"

A waiter came up to Bliss with several cocktail glasses on a tray. "Would you like a martini, Miss?"

"Yes," she said firmly, taking the glass.

"Don't be a damn fool, Bliss," Hunter said angrily. "You can't handle that stuff."

"Watch me." She took a big gulp. "Your trouble is you don't really know me."

"If that's true, then I'm the biggest chump on record," he muttered.

"We all make mistakes."

Bliss moved away, outwardly serene, but suffering inside. She'd given Hunter the impression that she was the rankest kind of opportunist. But it was no worse than having him consider her a naive child who couldn't think for herself. This way he had an excuse to wash his hands of her.

As though to prove his relief, Hunter didn't attempt to stop her. Clay didn't renew his assault, either. She saw him come back in the room a few minutes later, but he kept a discreet distance.

Bliss wasn't at a loss for company, however. She was surrounded by changing groups of people whose faces were all slightly blurred. Their conversation wasn't too clear, either, so she smiled a lot and nodded her head, which seemed to be adequate.

"Drink up so I can get you a refill," one of the men told her.

She hadn't touched the martini after the first swallow, but now she raised the glass and drained it obediently. Almost immediately the room started to twirl alarmingly. With a murmured excuse, Bliss left the men and headed for some tall French doors that she hoped led outside.

The cool night air didn't help a great deal. Now the patio furniture was swirling around. Suddenly an arm about her shoulders guided her down a path into the darkened garden.

"Just take it easy," Hunter's deep voice said soothingly. "You'll be okay."

"I don't feel very well," she answered piteously.

"I know, sweetheart." His voice held a hint of laughter. "It's an initiation we all go through."

He walked her up and down until some of the dizziness wore off. When she felt a little steadier, they sat on a bench by a tiled fountain with a naked cherub in the center.

Bliss tilted her head back. "Go ahead, say I told you so. You're entitled."

"I try never to repeat myself." He dipped a snowy handkerchief into the fountain, squeezed it out and put it on her forehead.

"Mmm, that feels good."

"You might not think so at the moment, but you're going to live." He chuckled.

"I'm not so sure I want to. How did you know I was sick?"

"I expected it so I was watching you, in spite of your instructions."

A small ray of happiness penetrated Bliss's distress. Either old habits died hard, or Hunter really cared what happened to her.

"I'm sorry about all those things I said," she told him. "None of them were true. Clay did give me a line about getting me into show business, but even in equatorial Africa we knew about snow jobs."

Hunter looked at her approvingly. "Maybe I didn't need to worry about you, after all."

She managed a wan smile. "Meaning I'm not as dumb as I look?"

"Nobody could ever consider you dumb, but your appearance tonight is deceiving." His eyes wandered over her elaborate coiffeur and sexy gown.

She sighed. "Who would ever think a hairdo could make that much difference? I've never been this popular."

"The dress might have something to do with it," he commented dryly.

The male look on his face encouraged Bliss. She looked up at him through long lashes. "Don't you like my dress?"

"I think it's smashing." He stood. "Come on, I'll take you home."

She curled up in Hunter's car with her head on his shoulder, as close to complete contentment as her queasy stomach would allow.

He brushed his cheek against her temple. "Feeling better?"

"A little." After a short silence she said, "I didn't tell you everything that happened tonight."

"Oh?"

"Clay's wife found us in his bedroom." As she felt Hunter's muscles tense, Bliss said hastily, "We were only talking, but he had dimmed the lights so I could see the view better."

"How thoughtful." Hunter's voice was heavy with sarcasm.

"I know that wasn't the reason, but we weren't doing anything wrong."

"That must have surprised Giselle."

"They said really horrid things to each other. How can they stay married, Hunter?"

"It's a symbiotic relationship—they're mutually useful to each other. She likes the money and prestige he gives her, and Clay likes the safety of marriage. He can tell all his little playmates that he's crazy about them, but his wife won't give him a divorce."

"That's disgusting!"

"It works for him," Hunter said ironically.

"But they must have loved each other when they got married. What happened? They have everything in the world."

"It's trite yet true—money doesn't buy happiness."

"Poverty doesn't, either. They don't know how lucky they are." Bliss yawned. "I'd like a shot a being that rich." She closed her eyes and burrowed deeper into Hunter's shoulder.

He didn't reply, but his expression was troubled as he gazed down at her delicate profile.

Bliss awoke feeling dizzy again when Hunter stopped the car in front of her apartment. "It was a mistake to close my eyes." She groaned.

He opened the passenger door and helped her out. "Do you want me to carry you?"

"No, I can walk. I've made enough of a spectacle of myself tonight."

Hunter smiled. "Only in front of me, and I can keep a secret."

"I'd appreciate that." When they reached her door she said, "Thanks for everything, Hunter. I won't forget this."

He unlocked the door and followed her inside. "I'll wait until you get into bed."

"I might simply collapse on top of it the way I am."

"You'll be more comfortable if you get undressed." He turned her around and unzipped the back of her gown, then gave her a light pat on the bottom. "Go on, scoot."

In the bedroom, Bliss stepped out of her dress slowly. Her skin tingled where his fingers had trailed down her back. Had Hunter meant his touch to be suggestive?

"Are you all right?" he called.

She stood perfectly still, undecided. Was he waiting for some signal from her?

"Answer me, Bliss. Are you in bed?" When she didn't respond he opened the door. "What are you—"

He stopped abruptly as the path of light illuminated her slender body, bare except for a pair of silk panties. His eyes moved in rapt fascination over her firm, up-tilted breasts, her slim hips, the long line of her slender legs. He was frozen, like a man entranced. Bliss made a tiny sound that broke the spell.

"Why are you standing there like that?" He pulled the spread off the bed and wrapped her in it before picking her up. "I told you to get into bed."

She struggled to get her arms out of the folds, then clasped them around his neck and pulled his head down.

"Stop it, Bliss! You don't know what you're—"

Her mouth covered his, cutting off all opposition. She acted out of intuition, twining her fingers in his hair while she tried to part his uncooperative lips.

Hunter's resistance was valiant, but futile. After a moment his arms tightened, and he became the aggressor. Clamping a hand around her nape, he plundered her mouth with his tongue, displaying a hunger that surpassed her own.

The knowledge that he wanted her filled Bliss with joy. She scattered tiny kisses over his face and neck while she unbuttoned his shirt, inciting him further.

"Oh, God, you have no idea what you're doing to me." He groaned.

"I love you, Hunter."

When she heard the words coming out of her mouth, Bliss knew she wasn't in full possession of her faculties, but it didn't matter. Nothing mattered except becoming a woman in the arms of the man who possessed her in every other way.

"You don't know what you're saying, sweetheart," he said regretfully.

When he tried to lower her to the bed she refused to relinquish her hold. In attempting to loosen her arms, he lost his balance and tumbled on top of her. Before he could get up, Bliss pulled his shirt aside and wound her arms around his torso. The sensation of their bare bodies meeting was like a jolt of electricity.

Hunter drew in his breath sharply. "Don't let me do this, Bliss."

She took his hand and put it around her breast. "I want you so much."

A shudder went through his long frame as he muttered, "Not half as much as I want you."

"Then love me, darling." Without giving him a chance to refuse she covered his mouth with hers.

Hunter's surrender was complete. He freed her from the tangled spread and looked down with eyes that lit up the darkness. A torrent of emotion raced through Bliss as he caressed her breasts with his fingertips, circling the sensitive nipples until she cried out with pleasure.

"Your body is so exquisite." He lowered his head to rub his cheek sensuously across her taut stomach. "Your skin is like warm velvet." He turned his head to dip his tongue into her navel.

Bliss's breathing quickened as he gently parted her legs while his mouth trailed lower. The seductive stroking on her inner thighs, coupled with his erotic kisses, was driving her into a frenzy. Her entire body was like an instrument being played by a master.

"I never felt this wild." She gasped. "Like I'm spinning out of control."

Hunter's hands suddenly bit into her thighs. His head remained lowered for a moment, then he sat back on his haunches and looked at her with controlled anger.

"I don't imagine you'll even remember this deplorable incident tomorrow. I only wish I could count on being as fortunate."

How could he call their need for each other a deplorable incident? "Don't do this to me again," she pleaded.

"You're drunk, Bliss," he said bluntly. "You don't know what you're doing."

"I do!"

He obviously didn't believe her. "This is twice you've almost made me lose my self-respect." He stared moodily down at her as he buttoned his shirt.

"Don't lie to me!" she flared. "Why don't you simply admit you have this mental block about virgins?"

"I have reservations about taking advantage of *any* woman who's had too much to drink," he answered grimly. "Go to bed and sleep it off, Bliss."

When she could think rationally, Bliss was glad Hunter thought all her actions stemmed from an unaccustomed martini. He was right about one thing, at least. Sober, she would never have confessed her love for him. Luckily he didn't believe her. Would it have made any difference if he had? No, she concluded sadly. It would be just one more strike against her.

Bliss slept almost a drugged sleep, whereas Hunter paced the floor a good part of the night. He wrestled with his problems until the early hours without finding a solution.

"I heard you walking about all night." Max set a glass of freshly squeezed orange juice in front of him the next morning. "What's wrong?"

"Nothing's wrong." Hunter opened the newspaper and started to read the baseball scores.

"Don't hand me that. You usually sleep like a baby."

"What do you know about babies?"

"They cry a lot and have disgusting toilet habits but everybody seems to like them. What's your point?"

Hunter sighed. "Could I just once read my paper without a lot of conversation?"

"Sure. Would it be considered conversation if I asked how you want your eggs?"

"I'll have cereal instead."

"Bacon doesn't go with cereal. I already made bacon."

"All right, I'll have scrambled eggs."

"I don't want you to feel pressured."

"Am I wrong, or are we having a conversation?" Hunter asked ironically.

"Not a very interesting one. What was bothering you last night?"

Hunter gave in, knowing he was no match for Max. "Something happened at Dennison's party that disturbed me."

"Are you going to tell me, or make me play Twenty Questions?"

"He made a move on Bliss."

"How did she take it?"

Hunter smiled faintly. "She was appalled that a married man would do such a thing."

"So what's the problem? He won't get to first base with her."

"No, but a *single* sleazeball might. They were all over her last night."

Max gave him an oblique look. "What do you expect? She's a living doll."

"She's also more naive than your average twelve-year-old."

"She had sense enough to tell Dennison to take a hike," Max observed.

"I'm not sure her heart was really in it. Bliss has the scruples of a missionary's daughter, but she isn't immune to temptation."

"What did she find tempting about him?"

"Not Clay, his way of life."

"So he's got a few more toys than most people. Big deal."

"It *could* be a big deal to someone who just found out what she's been missing all these years," Hunter said slowly.

"You're afraid she'll think it over and change her mind?"

"Not about Dennison."

"Then what's the problem?"

"She was different last night." Hunter scowled at his orange juice. "I didn't think she'd react that way. In spite of her sheltered existence, I thought her basic values were sound. But Clay's ostentatious monstrosity of a house impressed her, and she lapped up all the phony baloney those jerks were feeding her."

"So she enjoyed herself. That's not a crime. Just because you don't enjoy parties doesn't mean other people shouldn't."

"It was more than the party. She didn't even look the same." Hunter sighed. "I knew she'd change, but I didn't expect it to be so soon."

"What do you care?" Max asked casually. "She doesn't mean anything to you."

Hunter frowned. "I was the one who brought her into this. The least I can do is look out for her."

"You have a funny way of going about it. You don't spend any time with her."

"That doesn't have anything to do with it," Hunter said in annoyance. "She needs to meet other men."

"You said she did last night."

"The right kind of men."

"The kind that are interested in marriage?" Max asked innocently. "That would solve your problem. If she fell in love and got married you wouldn't have to worry about her anymore. Let's see, who's a likely candidate?"

"Aren't you a little old to be playing Cupid?" Hunter asked coldly.

"Hey, I care about Bliss, too. She's a terrific gal. I just wish you'd bring her around more often. Why don't you ask her over for dinner tonight?"

"I don't think she'd welcome hearing from me again," Hunter answered grimly.

"Why not? What did you do to her at that party?"

"I told her to sober up." Hunter pushed back his chair violently and went to stare out of the window with his fists jammed in his pockets. "Bliss got tipsy last night, something else I've never seen her do."

"That's not so terrible. Unless she took off her clothes and danced on top of a table, something I can't imagine Bliss doing." When Hunter continued to stare out at the garden, Max asked incredulously. "She didn't, did she?"

"No, of course not. I took her home. Nobody even knew."

"She's probably grateful to you, then."

Hunter smiled derisively. "I'm not counting on it."

Max looked at him shrewdly. "That's what really had you pacing the floor, isn't it? You put her to bed, and then forgot you were only being a Good Samaritan."

"I did not make love to her, damn it! What kind of a slug do you think I am?"

"But it bothers you that you wanted to. Why don't you stop fighting it and admit you're attracted to her?"

"All right, I'm attracted to her. Like any normal male, I find beautiful women appealing."

"Then why do you keep giving Bliss the cold shoulder?"

"For her own good," Hunter muttered.

"Get real. It's because you know she's in love with you, and it scares the hell out of you."

"She only thinks she's in love with me."

"In that case, you're not doing her any favor by playing hard to get," Max said craftily. "Everybody hankers after what they can't have. If you really wanted to discourage her, you'd take up all her time, hang around so much she'd get sick of you." He gazed at Hunter judiciously. "It shouldn't take long. You aren't all that charming."

"Thanks for the vote of confidence." Hunter stared at him thoughtfully. "I can see right through your Machiavellian scheming, but part of your advice is worth taking. I've left Bliss too much on her own. Last night showed me that. She needs me."

Max was careful to keep his voice bland. "Right on. You're the only one who doesn't want something from her. Why don't you phone her now?"

"She might still be asleep. I'll call her a little later."

Bliss woke with a splitting headache and a terrible taste in her mouth. When she started to get out of bed and discovered she was wearing only a pair of panties, the events of the previous night rushed back and she felt worse. How could she ever face Hunter again?

After two aspirin and a tall glass of water, she took a cold shower that revived her somewhat. She was putting on a bathrobe when the telephone rang.

"How are you feeling this morning?" Hunter's deep voice set all her nerves quivering.

She gripped the phone tightly and tried to match his normal tone. "Delicate, to put it mildly. I will never touch another drop of alcohol as long as I live, which probably won't be very much longer."

He laughed. "This, too, shall pass. I told you that last night."

"Was it during or after the party? I don't remember much about the evening," she said deliberately.

"I was hoping—I mean, I'm not surprised," he corrected himself quickly. "Do you remember that I took you home?"

"Only vaguely. I hope I could walk. You didn't have to prop me up or anything, did you?"

"No, you were navigating on your own."

"That's a relief. I only hope I can do the same today. Then all I have to do is make sense when I get to Roger's office."

"You don't have to go to work. Why don't we both take the day off and drive down to the beach? The fresh air will do you good."

"Roger is expecting me," she said doubtfully.

"He has plenty of material to work on."

She hesitated. "I don't think it's a very good idea, Hunter."

"Why not? We can talk about the script, if that will ease your conscience. Come on," he coaxed. "I don't feel like working today, and I know you don't."

His invitation was so out of the blue that she was at a loss for words. Even hearing from Hunter again was surprising. Did he call to find out if last night would be a problem between them? She blessed her unexpected acting ability. They couldn't have been friends if he hadn't believed her.

"How about it, Bliss?"

Her spirits suddenly lifted. "All right, as long as you take the blame if Roger complains."

"He won't. I'm the one who hired him. I'll pick you up in an hour."

Chapter Eight

Bliss was ready before the hour was up, so she decided to visit with Shelley while she was waiting for Hunter to arrive. The landlady was sitting in her accustomed spot on the patio.

"How was the party?" Shelley greeted her.

"It was all right."

"Is that the best you can do? It must have been a real bomb."

"No, it was...very interesting." Bliss knew more was expected from her or Shelley would ask probing questions. "I was absolutely fascinated by the house. It has every gadget ever invented."

"I can imagine. Who was there? Did you meet lots of celebrities?"

"Some, but mostly the press."

"Oh, it was one of *those* things. No wonder you're not raving. Was your friend Roger there, at least?"

"I didn't see him." Bliss glanced toward the street, waiting for a glimpse of Hunter's red Ferrari.

"Aren't you kind of late this morning?" Shelley asked.

"I'm not working today."

"If you're at loose ends you can come to the gym with me, but you'll have to take your own car. I'm not coming home."

"Another date with David?"

"No."

Shelley wasn't usually that taciturn. Bliss guessed the reason behind her brief answer, but she didn't take the hint. "Somebody new?" she asked innocently.

"I'm meeting Kirk." When Bliss didn't respond, Shelley said with a trace of belligerence, "Just because I went out with David a couple of times doesn't mean I dumped Kirk."

"Oh? I haven't seen his car around lately." Kirk drove an old but flashy sports car that couldn't be missed.

"He's been busy this past week making a commercial."

"That must be interesting work," Bliss observed politely, without pointing out that people didn't usually work day *and* night.

"I know what you're thinking." Shelley sighed. "Why do I keep taking him back? Kirk is a womanizer and a sponger. I pay his bills, and he cheats on me behind my back." She stood and paced the length of the patio. "I've tried to break it off, but when I see him again I defrost like a TV dinner in a microwave. Some men have that effect on a woman."

"I know," Bliss answered soberly.

"Kirk is weak, but he isn't really a bad person," Shelley said earnestly. "Women do throw themselves at him. It isn't all his fault. I believe him when he says he loves me.''

Bliss didn't know what to say. "I guess that's the important thing,'' she replied lamely.

Shelley sensed her reservations. "You ought to know something about obsession. You're hooked on a guy who's bad news, too.''

"I wouldn't say I was obsessed by Hunter,'' Bliss protested.

"Oh, no? You forgive him his trespasses and come back for more, exactly the way I do.''

Hunter chose that inopportune moment to arrive. As the powerful car nosed into the curb, Shelley smiled. "So that's why you didn't go to work today. I rest my case.''

Bliss's face was troubled as she and Hunter drove away. Was Shelley right? To compare Hunter to Kirk was insulting, but the end result was the same. Maybe he *had* become a compulsion. What else could explain her presence here today after their traumatic parting last night?

He covered her clenched fist with his big hand. "Head still pounding?''

"No, I feel almost human again.''

"Then what's bothering you, honey?''

"Nothing, really. I was talking to Shelley. She has problems.''

"You can't let other people's troubles get you down.''

"I know, but it's depressing to see a bright, capable woman throw herself away on a jerk. Why do women fall in love with the wrong men?'' she asked heatedly.

"Or vice versa.'' Hunter returned both hands to the wheel. "Falling in love isn't a matter of choice. It's like catching a cold. You can't avoid it, and there's no cure.''

"But the discomfort goes away eventually?" she asked in a small voice.

"That's always been my experience," he answered evenly.

Which meant that even if a miracle occurred and Hunter fell in love with her, he wouldn't expect it to last. Bliss wished that forecast applied to her.

Hunter changed the subject. "Do you want to go to the beach, or would you rather take a drive up the coast?"

"Let's go to the beach. I feel like walking."

"I think it would do you good," he agreed, glancing at her wan face.

Hunter bypassed the more popular spots like Wavecrest and Malibu in favor of a stretch of coastline that was almost like a private beach. Large rocks offshore made swimming and surfing hazardous, so the place was deserted except for a man fishing at the water's edge.

The took off their shoes and walked along the wet sand, leaving footprints that the foaming wavelets erased behind them. The sun beat down from a clear blue sky, but a light breeze kept the heat from being excessive.

"Does this bring back memories?" Hunter asked with a touch of concern.

"Not really. I didn't have anyone to keep me company when I walked on the beach."

"You won't ever be alone again." His voice was husky as he twined his fingers with hers.

Bliss knew that didn't mean what she wanted it to, but she left her hand in his. "Roger said we'll be living on a yacht when we go to the island."

He nodded. "I'm arranging it now, although we won't be going on location for at least a month. The early scenes will be shot on a soundstage, probably in about a week.''

"So soon? I haven't even seen the script yet. You promised I could object to anything that really bothered me," she reminded him.

"I have a rough draft with me. We can go over it this afternoon."

"How can Roger finish up in a week?"

"Writers are used to working under tight deadlines when they do television. Many of us, like Mona, have other commitments waiting."

"I feel much better about her doing the part since we spent that day together. She's a lot different than she looks."

"Mona is a great gal." Hunter smiled appreciatively. "A lot of people misjudge her. She's really a warm, generous woman."

This time Bliss withdrew her hand. "Could I see the script now?"

"If you like, but it's such a beautiful day. Why don't we take a ride to Santa Barbara, and then go back to my house? You can look it over in comfort without worrying about the pages blowing away."

It sounded like a delaying action. "Is there something in there you think I won't like?"

Hunter smiled wryly. "I can never predict your reactions. I gather you'd prefer to look at the script now."

She hesitated. "No, I guess it can wait."

Bliss was happy with her decision as they drove along the scenic coast. There was a very good chance they would clash over certain points in the script, and she wanted to prolong their present rapport as long as possible. This was almost like the old times when they had fun together without any sexual tension. Last night might never have happened.

Hunter glanced over and noticed her wistful smile. "Is something funny?"

"I was thinking about the day you took me to buy the car."

"Don't remind me! I got my first gray hairs that day."

"You didn't have to make me tell you what streets I'd be taking from then on," she teased. "I felt like I was filing a flight plan."

"That adequately describes your driving. Kamikaze pilots could take lessons from you."

They bantered back and forth on the way to Santa Barbara, a dignified small town with a beautiful old hotel and broad, tree-lined streets.

When Bliss commented on the air of tranquility, Hunter said, "Scarcely the kind of place you'd expect teenagers to pick for a special occasion. But after grad night in L.A., the thing to do was drive to Santa Barbara for breakfast. Don't ask me why. This is a long way to go for scrambled eggs, but we could say we stayed up all night. It was a youthful rite of passage."

"That's tame. We went on a lion hunt with wooden spears to celebrate our adulthood."

"You're joking!"

She laughed at the shocked look on his face. "Yes, I'm joking. I was only trying to one-up you. I didn't expect you to believe me."

"Nothing you do would surprise me," he declared.

The sun was setting when they reached the outskirts of Los Angeles. "Now we'll go to my house and get down to work," Hunter said.

"It would make more sense to go to my apartment instead, as long as you have the script with you. Then you won't have to bring me back."

"That wouldn't be a hardship."

"I'd still rather go home."

She suspected that Hunter's reluctance was due to the events of the previous night, but this was one way of convincing him that she didn't remember them.

"If that's what you want," he finally agreed, a trifle grimly.

Bliss offered him the newspaper to read while she was going over the manuscript, but he said, "Don't worry about me. I'll use the time to make a few phone calls."

After picking up the messages from his answering service, Hunter had more than a few calls to return. Everyone seemed to have a problem that only he could solve.

Bliss was finished before he was. When he hung up after the last call she said, "Can't anyone make a decision without you?"

"It's my job to pull everything together."

"Do you always have so many crises at the end of the day?"

"They usually come up singly, but I wasn't around today."

"You really couldn't afford the time, could you? Why did you take the day off to be with me, Hunter?"

"You've just answered your own question." Something glowed briefly in his eyes before being carefully veiled. "Dennison had given you a bad time, and the party was a washout, more of an extended news conference, actually. I didn't want you to get tied up in knots over it."

"You're probably the nicest man I'll ever meet," she said slowly.

He glossed over the compliment gracefully. "I hope you'll think so after we discuss the script. Any problems with it so far?"

"Not many. Roger did a good job, but he left out a few things. The meeting of the tribal chieftains where Dad was honored is one of them. I'm also a little unhappy about his treatment of the fertility rites."

"Okay." Hunter made notes on a pad of paper. "What else?"

When she'd aired all her reservations, they discussed them. Most of the time Hunter conceded the point, but in some cases he explained why the limits of time made certain shortcuts necessary. It was almost eight o'clock when they finally reached total accord. After glancing at his watch, Hunter expressed surprise at the hour.

"I hope I didn't make you late for something," Bliss said.

"No, I only planned to watch a program on TV. I want to check out the performance of one of the actors. Do you mind if I watch it here? The show would be half over by the time I got home."

"I don't mind at all."

"Don't let me keep you from anything. If you're going out I can lock up when I leave."

"I didn't have any plans. Hurry up and turn on the set or you'll miss the beginning."

It gave Bliss a warm, domestic feeling to see Hunter relaxed on her sofa watching television. Before letting herself get carried away, she went into the kitchen to fill a small bowl with salted peanuts.

Hunter gave her an abstracted smile when she placed the bowl on a small table next to him. But from the way he immediately started to devour the contents, she knew he was hungry.

He patted the cushion beside him without taking his eyes from the screen. "Come watch with me."

"In a minute. I have something to do first." It was unlikely that Hunter had another date since the show wouldn't be over until nine, so Bliss had decided to make dinner.

The contents of the refrigerator weren't encouraging. Cooking for one person never seemed worth the effort. She usually fixed a salad or made a sandwich when she was alone. That would scarcely satisfy a hungry man, however.

Ingenuity was clearly called for. She took cans of tuna, mushroom soup and Chinese noodles from the cupboard, and a package of green peas from the freezer. With deft motions she diced celery, minced onions and sliced water chestnuts. After all the ingredients were combined in a casserole and placed in the oven, she went back to the living room.

"Where have you been? You missed half the show," Hunter complained. "I don't know if I can explain the plot to you."

"Don't bother, I'll catch on. All the action takes place in the last ten minutes, anyway."

"Don't tell that to our sponsors. We like them to think people remain glued to their seats."

Bliss couldn't have cared less what the drama was about. She was content merely to sit beside Hunter and enjoy his presence, even though his attention was elsewhere.

When the show was over she asked, "Did you like it?"

"Not particularly. I only watched it for Malcolm Taylor's performance. He was the second lead. I'm interested in him for my next project."

"We've barely started the documentary."

"These things are planned long in advance. You have to sign the people you want or they'll be unavailable." He stared at Bliss without really seeing her, his eyes lit with enthusiasm. "I'm going to contact Taylor's agent first thing in the morning. He's perfect for the part I have in mind."

Bliss felt a moment's resentment. Hunter had never shown that much fervor about doing *her* story. Before she could mention the fact, he sniffed the air appreciatively.

"Something smells wonderful."

"I'm making dinner. It should be almost ready."

"You didn't have to do that, honey. I would have taken you out."

"It wasn't any trouble. Just don't expect anything fancy," she warned.

"Whatever you make will be fine. I could eat two helpings of anything right now."

"That's not exactly high anticipation."

He laughed. "It wasn't very complimentary, I agree. What can I do to make up for it?"

"You can set the table while I put the biscuits in the oven."

Hunter followed her into the kitchen. "Judging by the aroma, you must be a good cook."

"A limited one, I'm afraid. Tuna casserole is one of the few things I know how to make—that you'd eat, anyway," she added with a grin.

"Don't try to spoil my appetite with stories about roasted grasshoppers and the like. I'm on to your tall tales."

"You wouldn't believe I caught frogs as big as footballs in the lagoon?"

"A frog that big would have to be suffering from an overactive thyroid," he scoffed.

"Would you like to make a little bet?"

"You're on! But we'll keep the stakes low. I don't want to take your money."

"It doesn't have to be money. A written apology will do. I intend to frame it," she said smugly.

"*If* you win. First I have to see these monsters with my own eyes. I'd like to have a picture of one."

"You're making conditions," Bliss complained. "They only come out at night."

"A likely story. Now who's trying to get out of the bet?" he crowed.

"Okay, there's only one way to settle this. Are you willing to spend a night on the island when we get there? I'll even let you bring a sleeping bag," she said with a touch of condescension.

He picked it up immediately. "You don't have to make any concessions for me. I can rough it if you can."

She smiled. "We'll see." The timer on the oven rang, putting an end to the dispute. "Sit down, dinner's ready."

Hunter did ample justice to the simple meal. The casserole dish was almost empty, and only one biscuit remained on the plate when he finally put his fork down with a contented sigh.

"I wish you'd give Max this recipe. It was great."

"He'd be insulted that you enjoyed anyone's cooking but his."

"I'm sure he'd make an exception in your case. You've made a conquest."

They were lingering over coffee when the telephone on the kitchen wall rang, startling both of them. Clay Dennison's voice was a further surprise.

"I'm sorry to be calling so late," he said. "I hope I'm not disturbing you."

"No." She glanced over at Hunter, who was pretending not to listen.

"You weren't in the office today, and I couldn't get you at home," Clay was explaining. "Then I got tied up. Otherwise I would have called earlier."

"It's quite all right. What can I do for you?"

"That's a very provocative question from such a beautiful lady," he answered playfully.

"I'm sure you know what I mean."

When he detected the coolness in her voice his manner became businesslike. "I've been considering the possibility of having you make a special appearance at the end of the documentary. You could deliver a little speech about how happy you are that your life story has been portrayed so faithfully."

"That wasn't part of our agreement," she answered slowly.

"We didn't happen to talk about it, but your contract doesn't say you *won't* appear."

"Only because it never came up. If it had, I would have said no."

"I'm disappointed in you, Bliss. You don't seem like the kind of person who thinks only of herself."

"I'm not," she protested. "It's simply that I hate being in the spotlight. I'd be terribly nervous."

"I understand." His voice had the soothing tone of an indulgent uncle. "But I'm sure we could make it painless for you. Why don't we discuss the idea?"

"All right," she said, to end the argument and gain time.

"Excellent. Suppose I send a car for you. We'll have a nice relaxing drink and come to an agreement you can live with."

"You mean now?" she asked in astonishment.

"Why not? We might as well get everything settled."

Bliss got the picture belatedly. "Isn't the office locked at this hour?"

"Well, actually, I'm at home, but that's no problem. We can meet here just as well. Better, in fact. There won't be as many disturbances."

Certainly not by his wife, who could be counted on not to appear, for one reason or another. "I don't know, Clay," she said deliberately.

Hunter had been listening openly for some moments, his expression increasingly stormy. He stood abruptly and strode toward her.

"Maybe I should talk to Hunter first," she finished.

"That won't be necessary," Clay said smoothly. "I'm sure we can put our heads together and come up with a solution that will satisfy both of us."

"I wouldn't want Hunter to think I was going behind his back."

Dennison's urbanity slipped a trifle. "I don't like having to remind you of the fact, but I *am* president of WBC."

"But I believe Hunter has creative control. Why don't you talk it over with him yourself? He's right here." She handed the phone to Hunter before Clay could object.

"What's going on?" Hunter demanded.

"This is a surprise." Dennison's tone didn't indicate it was a pleasant one.

"What are you trying to get Bliss to do?"

"We can talk about it tomorrow. It was just an idea I had."

"I know about your ideas. They're out of line in this case."

"Well, hell, why didn't you tell me you were playing house with her?" Dennison sounded aggrieved. "I thought she was up for grabs."

A muscle bunched at the point of Hunter's strong jaw, but he kept his voice even. "You should have gotten a clue from the way I negotiated her contract."

"I thought it was personal satisfaction, knowing how you love to give me the shaft."

"Not this time." Hunter's eyes were enigmatic as he gazed at Bliss.

"Okay, I'll back off. She's all yours, you lucky dog."

"Thanks a lot," Hunter answered mockingly.

Bliss had been listening to his end of the conversation. When he hung up she said, "That was short. What did he say?"

"In essence, that he won't bother you anymore. That *is* what you want, isn't it?"

"Of course! But how did you manage to discourage him when I couldn't?"

Hunter smiled thinly. "I used different arguments."

"You told him we were . . . that I was your girlfriend, didn't you?"

"It was the only thing short of a land mine that would have stopped him. Clay is very single-minded when he targets a woman."

"It's nice to know there's honor among Casanovas," she remarked disdainfully.

Hunter's eyes narrowed dangerously. "Are you putting me in his class?"

"No, certainly not," she answered quickly. "I only meant that I'm glad he has *some* ethics, even if they're not admirable."

"I'm sorry if you're uncomfortable about having him think we're involved," Hunter said quietly.

"I don't really care what he thinks. It could be more of a problem for you if Clay spreads the rumor. You might have some explaining to do in certain quarters." She tried to make the comment sound amused.

"Never explain, never complain." Hunter matched her light tone. "Or is it the other way around?"

"I'm never sure myself, but I don't suppose it matters as long as you don't do either one."

Their attempt at lighthearted repartee fell flat. Clay's phone call had changed the whole mood of the evening. After a short time Hunter said he had to leave.

"Thanks for dinner. It was excellent."

"I'm glad you enjoyed it. Thank *you* for a nice day."

They were being so polite to each other that Bliss could have cried. Whenever Hunter felt he was committing himself, he retreated behind a wall of formality. Would she ever find a chink in that wall? With a feeling of hopelessness, she went into the kitchen to wash the dishes.

After reading manuscript pages for hours the next morning, Bliss told Roger, "I need a coffee break. Do you have time to come with me?"

"Sure. I'm just about finished with the rewrite, which is good news since we start shooting on Monday."

Hunter came out of his office as they were passing by. "Where are you two off to?" he asked.

"We're on a break," Roger said. "Care to come with us to the commissary?"

"I could use a cup of coffee. I didn't have any this morning."

Roger grinned. "Was Max sulking?"

"No, he was in a good mood for once. I just over-slept." Hunter looked at Bliss. "Is everything okay? No more phone calls."

She shook her head. "Not a jingle."

"Have you been getting obscene phone calls?" Roger said.

"I wouldn't exactly call them that." She smiled.

"I would," Hunter said curtly as the elevator door opened.

They talked about the script while they walked to the commissary. On the way to a table, the men stopped a couple of times to speak to co-workers. They were standing near the door when Clay Dennison came in with one of his many assistants.

Bliss expected him to continue on to the private dining room reserved for VIPs. Clay never sat with the workers. Instead of walking by, however, he came over to their group.

"Glad you made it in this morning, Hunter," he said jovially, his eyes sliding to Bliss. Roger was ignored.

"Did you want to see me about something?" Hunter asked without reacting to the barb.

"I thought you might want to give me a progress report," Clay answered smoothly.

"I prefer to let my record speak for itself."

"There's such a thing as being overconfident."

Hunter smiled mockingly. "You should know."

The eyes of the two men clashed for an instant. Then the studio chief regained his poise. Turning to Bliss he remarked, "I suppose you're looking forward to tonight."

She gave him a puzzled stare. "What happens tonight?"

"Aren't you taking Bliss to the Gold Seal Awards?" he asked Hunter.

"Well . . . actually, I'm taking Mona," Hunter explained reluctantly. "She needed an escort."

"I see." Dennison was delighted by his discomfort. "Too bad you'll have to miss the most prestigious event of the year," he told Bliss. "I thought surely Hunter had asked you, or I wouldn't have mentioned it."

"That's all right, I don't mind." Bliss hoped she sounded convincing, because she minded very much. Not missing the gala—the fact that Hunter was taking Mona.

"Where do you find them this understanding?" Dennison asked Hunter. "If you were my girlfriend, Bliss, *I'd* take you," he said, pretending it was a joke.

A waitress approached them. "Did you want a table, Mr. Dennison?"

"No, I'm going into the dining room. Well, I'll see you all later." He walked away with a satisfied expression.

"Clay thought he was being funny," Bliss said hastily as Roger looked speculatively at her and Hunter.

Before she could try to convince him of the fact, someone called Roger over to another table. "Order me a jelly doughnut," he said. "I'll join you in a couple of minutes."

"I told you Clay would spread rumors," Bliss said when she and Hunter were seated.

"Not necessarily. He was just trying to make trouble between us. Roger simply happened to be there."

"You really dislike each other, don't you?"

"That's pretty obvious."

"Then how can you work for him, and why would he hire you? Max said Clay dangled offers in front of you for months before you accepted this one."

"It isn't obligatory to like the people you work with. What really matters is a person's ability to get the job done. Dennison puts up with me because I have a proven track record. He knows I'll make money for him."

"And what would make you put up with *him*? I can't believe it's solely money. You're too independent."

"We all have our price," he answered somberly.

"I'm glad for my own sake, but was it worth it to you?"

"I thought so at the time." He stared at her with a mixture of emotions.

"But now you don't"

"I wouldn't say that. Dennison is no bargain, but life is filled with compromise. I do have one regret, however."

That he met her and complicated his life? When he didn't go on, she asked in a muted voice, "Does your regret involve me?"

Hunter's expression changed as he gazed at her troubled face. "Not the way you think. You're the silver lining in a cloudy sky."

Bliss was immensely gratified by the compliment, delivered in the husky voice that always made her pulse beat faster. She never found out what his one regret was, though. The waitress arrived to take their order, and Roger came back a moment later.

Conversation didn't flow as easily between the three of them as it had before Clay made his insinuation. Roger seemed a little uncomfortable, as though he didn't know quite how to treat her now, and Hunter was withdrawn. They didn't linger over coffee.

Bliss arrived home at the end of the day feeling vaguely depressed. It was Friday, and she didn't have any plans for the weekend. Ironically, Roger considered her off-limits because of Hunter, who wasn't interested. Hunter might possibly call—he was very unpredictable—but she wasn't counting on it.

The phone rang, reviving her spirits in a flash. They drooped again when Max's voice greeted her instead of Hunter's.

"How's it going, kid?" he asked.

"Okay, I guess."

"That good, huh?" he asked dryly.

"No, really. Everything's fine." She forced herself to sound cheerful. "How's your poker? Are you taking them to the cleaners?"

"You've got that right. I'm awesome."

Bliss smiled. "I already know that. I wouldn't want to compete with you."

"You came out pretty good last night. The boss told me you fed him royally."

"It was only tuna casserole," she said deprecatingly.

"How about that? All these years and I never knew he liked tuna casserole. I'll tell you what he's crazy about, though. The boss goes ape over chili and beans. I open cans of chili, top them with grated cheese and chopped onions, and he thinks I've been cooking all afternoon. Try it next time he comes to dinner," Max said casually. "He'll think you're Julia Child."

"I'll keep it in mind, but I don't know when that will be," Bliss answered a trifle forlornly. "Last night was just a fluke."

"Well, you never know. If I were you I'd buy a couple of cans of chili, just in case."

"I'll do that," she promised, more to end the conversation than anything else.

As she hung up, Shelley walked by. Bliss ran to the window. "Would you like to come in for coffee?" she called.

"Come over to my house for something stronger."

Bliss accepted the invitation gratefully, but when they reached Shelley's apartment she declined a drink.

"Does it have something to do with being a missionary's daughter?" Shelley asked curiously.

"Nothing like that. I . . . ah . . . I'm on a diet."

"Aren't we all?" Shelley poured herself a Scotch, nonetheless, and gave Bliss a diet cola.

"Would you like to go to a movie after work?" Bliss asked.

"I'm not working tonight. I want to catch the Gold Seal Awards. Stay and watch with me if you're at loose ends," Shelley said, switching on the set.

A television personality was interviewing celebrities as they arrived at the theater in a long procession of limousines. Glamorous women and handsome men were greeted by screams of approval from the crowds restrained behind velvet ropes. The more famous stars were summoned to the microphone to say a few words that bore an unfailing resemblance.

"They all say the same thing," Bliss complained.

"That's because writers aren't putting words in their mouths. You're supposed to look, not listen." Shelley's eyes gleamed. "I'd mortgage my studio for a gown like that. It must have cost thousands."

They watched the spectacle, comparing the outfits and commenting on the elaborate hairdos. Bliss was enjoying herself until Mona stepped out of a stretch limo to be greeted by wild cheers from onlookers. Hunter came in for his share of adulation even though it was doubtful that many people recognized him. He was wildly handsome in a darkly brooding way, and his excellently tailored dinner clothes showed off a superb physique. That was enough.

"I don't have to introduce Mona Jensen to any of you," the man with the mike said. "Come over and say a few words to your fans, Mona. Doesn't she look gorgeous, folks?"

That was an understatement. Mona was dressed in white from head to toe. Her Grecian-style, long silk gown was topped by a full-length white fox cape, and diamonds sparkled at her ears and on both wrists.

After she told everyone how thrilled she was to be there, the man held out the microphone to Hunter, who was standing out of the spotlight.

"Mona's escort this evening is the well-known producer, Hunter Lord. Say hello to our television audience, Mr. Lord."

Hunter smiled and shook his head, turning to talk to friends.

The emcee took the rejection in stride, his enthusiasm undampened. "I guess Mr. Lord is in a hurry to get inside. Thanks for visiting with us, Mona. And now, here comes Francesca Colby, that sexy siren of *The Young Rebels*."

With a final smile to the crowd, Mona rejoined Hunter. Whatever she said made him laugh and put his arm around her. The gesture was innocent enough. It was the look on his face as he gazed down at her that chilled Bliss.

Shelley was too engrossed in the newest arrival to notice. "I wonder who did her hair. The guy must have practiced on circus clowns. Did you ever see such a mess?"

When Bliss didn't respond, she glanced over at her, then back to the screen. Hunter was leading Mona into the theater, still with his arm around her.

"They're certainly a couple of pros," Shelley remarked casually. "These things are all a big hype, you know. It's good publicity for the show to give the impression that they're an item."

"Does Hunter look like he's acting?" Bliss asked bitterly.

Shelley hesitated, but directness was her nature. "Okay, so I was trying to make you feel better. Maybe you'd be better off finding yourself another guy before this one breaks your heart."

"It's a little late for that," Bliss said forlornly.

"I kind of thought so. Well, if that's the case, stop moping around and really go after him."

"Compete with Mona?"

"Why not? You've been up against long odds before and you came through."

The reminder was riveting. She *had* won out when the deck was stacked against her. How could she even consider handing Hunter over without a struggle?

"You're absolutely right." She gave Shelley a gallant smile. "After all, what does Mona have that I don't? Except more of it."

"Right on," Shelley said approvingly.

Chapter Nine

Bliss couldn't wait to put her campaign into action the next morning. She'd planned just what to say, and how to act. It was a blow to discover that Hunter had gone away for the weekend.

"He's out scouting locations for his next project," Max informed her.

"That seems to interest him a lot more than the one he's working on now," she commented, not bothering to hide her disappointment.

"I wouldn't say that. The boss is a Superman. Even when his attention is divided, he can still give his all to whatever he's working on at the moment."

Or *whoever*, Bliss thought darkly. She refused to be discouraged, however. Her day would come.

Bliss waited impatiently for Monday morning. Anticipation was running through her veins as she drove to the studio where Hunter had rented facilities. She would have him all to herself today, since Mona wasn't in the early scenes.

Soundstage *C* was housed in a huge structure that resembled an airplane hangar. Dozens of people were milling about talking, while workmen pushed various pieces of equipment around. In the rather dim lighting, Bliss almost tripped over a large cable that was curled on the floor like a snake.

She looked in vain for Hunter, or at least a friendly face, but nobody paid any attention to her. Finally, she asked a man in jeans and a plaid shirt if he knew where Hunter was.

"Wouldn't know him if I saw him. Ask Rafe Grantland, he's the director." He pointed out a short, balding man, also in jeans.

He was surrounded by people, and Bliss hesitated to interrupt. But when that seemed the only way to get his attention, she said, "Excuse me. Can you tell me where to find Hunter Lord?"

"I'd like to know myself. Joe!" he bellowed to a man on a high scaffold. "How soon will those lights be hooked up? We haven't got all day."

As he started to walk away, Bliss said a trifle desperately, "You *are* expecting him, aren't you?"

"Listen, lady, I've got a movie to shoot. You'll have to keep out of the way or get off the set."

Her jawline firmed. "*You* listen. I'm Bliss Goodwin, and I have a right to be here."

The change in him was dramatic. After apologizing for his rudeness he led her to a canvas chair in front of a facsimile of a living room. Giant cameras faced the set where a couple in their forties were going over scripts.

"Shirley, Bill, come over here for a minute," the director called. "These are the actors who play your parents," he told Bliss.

While they were all chatting together pleasantly, a small girl with long blond hair joined them. She was about nine years old, but her self-possession was that of an adult.

"Hello, I'm Melissa Blaine. You're Bliss Goodwin, aren't you? I'm playing you as a child." She tipped her head to regard Bliss appraisingly. "We kind of look alike. I think it was very good casting, don't you?"

"You were an excellent choice," Bliss said gravely, concealing her amusement.

"I got the part over almost fifty other girls," Melissa said complacently.

Powerful klieg lights suddenly lit up the set, leaving the rest of the cavernous building in semidarkness. The actors took their places and the cameras began to roll.

Bliss was fascinated by the whole proceedings at first, but it became slightly boring after a while. The actual shooting lasted only a short time, and the same segment was filmed over and over again.

Everything was going smoothly, when suddenly a crisis arose. An assistant came over to Rafe with a message that made the volatile director erupt.

"Well, get someone else! What do you want me to do, send flowers?"

"They're trying to locate another teacher, but they don't know how long it will take," the assistant said nervously.

"Why me, oh Lord?" Rafe rolled his eyes to the ceiling. "Anyone who works with kids should have his head examined!"

Melissa had been listening along with everybody else. "Did something happen to Miss Thompson?" she asked.

"She was in an automobile accident on the way over here," he answered glumly. "Nothing serious, but she'll be out of commission for at least a week. You might as well all take an extended lunch," he announced, raising his voice for everyone to hear. "Be back on the set by three."

Since it was only a little after eleven, Bliss was astonished. "Is that all you're going to do this morning?"

"It's all we *can* do," Rafe said. "Child actors are covered by laws. They can only work a certain amount of hours, and you have to give them time off for school and lunch. By the time we get a substitute teacher over here—*if* we can get one—we've blown four hours."

It was all very complicated, but Bliss zeroed in on the pertinent part. "If she had a teacher you could save some of that time?"

"And thousands of dollars." He nodded.

"I'm a teacher. Will I do?"

"I realize you're trying to be helpful, Miss Goodwin, but we need a real teacher."

"I have college credentials," she answered crisply.

"No fooling?" Rafe looked hopeful for a moment before doubt set in. "We might get in trouble with the union, although it's their failure to deliver. Oh, hell, let's go for it! Change of plans, everybody," he shouted. "Let's start setting up again."

Melissa took Bliss to the schoolroom on the lot. It was only about the size of a small office, but it had a blackboard, a map of the world on one wall and several desks and chairs.

"The kids will be impressed when I tell them you were my teacher," Melissa confided. "I go to regular school when I'm not working."

"Do you like being an actress?" Bliss asked curiously.

"Sometimes I get bored and I'd rather play with my friends, but my mother tells me how lucky I am. Did your mother make you be a teacher?"

Bliss felt pity for the child, and renewed affection for her own parents. "No, that was my own choice," she said gently.

"Maybe I'll be a teacher when I grow up," Melissa remarked thoughtfully. "Or maybe a bareback rider in a circus. I know how to ride a horse."

Bliss laughed. "Right now let's see how much you know about geography."

After the lesson was over she took Melissa to the commissary for lunch. They were waiting for a table when Hunter joined them.

"Rafe told me how you came to the rescue," he said to Bliss.

"Just a lucky happenstance," she replied.

"It was more than that. You saved us a tidy sum. Delays are costly, and we don't like to start in the red."

"I expect you to be properly grateful," she remarked provocatively.

"You can name your reward," he answered, his eyes holding hers.

Melissa tugged at Bliss's hand. "He's handsome," she whispered audibly. "Is he your boyfriend?"

Bliss looked at Hunter with a smile that matched his. "Yes," she answered deliberately.

"I have a boyfriend, too," Melissa informed him.

"I hope he's not the jealous type, because I'd like to join you and Miss Goodwin for lunch," Hunter said.

"You're just teasing me." Melissa giggled. "I can tell you're in love with *her*."

"I didn't know it was that obvious," he answered lightly.

Melissa's adult comments entertained them throughout lunch, but after they had delivered her back to the set Bliss said, "Poor little kid, I feel sorry for her."

"A number of stage mothers would commit mayhem for the part Melissa has," Hunter observed dryly.

"That's just the point. The children don't choose this as a career. Their mothers are simply fulfilling their own ambitions."

"Unfortunately that's often true, but there are laws to safeguard minors."

"Would you push your child into a career in show business?" she demanded.

"I'd probably forbid it, which is almost as bad. If we ever have children you don't need to worry about that," he teased.

"You'll have to marry me first," she said boldly.

Hunter's expression altered. "I keep forgetting you're a missionary's daughter." He changed the subject, none too smoothly. "Would you consider filling in until Melissa's regular teacher returns? She likes you, and it would be less of a disruption for her."

"I'd enjoy it very much. It might give me local credentials if I ever get accredited."

"You haven't changed your mind about teaching?"

"Not at all. That's my chosen field."

"You seem so interested in moviemaking," he answered slowly.

"Most people would be. But it's like Disneyland—a fun place to visit, but who would want to live there?" She smiled. "No offense intended."

"None taken. Actually, I'm delighted. I thought you'd changed."

"I have." She looked thoughtful. "I don't know if it's good or bad, but I'm becoming more assertive."

"That's a necessity in this town." He chuckled.

"Hunter, can I see you over here for a minute?" Rafe called.

Hunter left her briefly. When he returned, he said, "I'm sorry, but I have to leave."

"I have a few things to do, too," she said. "I'll walk out with you."

The bright sunshine outside was a vivid contrast to the artificiality of the stage lighting. They blinked as their eyes adjusted to the glare.

"I saw you on television the other night," Bliss remarked casually. "Mona looked stunning."

"That's part of being a star."

"She has a lot to work with, though."

"Mona is a natural beauty even without makeup," he admitted.

Bliss's heart plunged like a stone. "I guess she's the kind of woman no man ever gets out of his system," she said hopelessly.

"If you're referring to me, I've told you before that Mona and I are just good friends." Hunter's voice held a touch of impatience. "She's very involved with a television actor named Cullen Wainwright."

Bliss knew from Hunter's manner that she should let the matter drop, but she couldn't. Was jealousy to blame for his annoyance?

"He must be a very secure person not to mind her going out with other men," she commented.

"Cullen is shooting an episode of a TV series in Las Vegas. That's why Mona asked me to be her escort at the awards thing."

Bliss was unconvinced. That didn't account for their behavior together, the shared intimacy that spoke volumes. She would have felt better if he'd used Shelley's excuse about drumming up publicity for the show.

They had reached Bliss's car. She unlocked the door, giving him a bright smile. "Well, I'll see you around."

Hunter stared at her with indecision. "If I'd thought you wanted to go the other night I would have gotten tickets for you and Roger."

That was the final insult. Bliss wanted to tell him to stop fixing her up like someone's homely cousin from Hicksville, but pride prevented her.

"I couldn't have gone, anyway," she said. "I had a date with a really interesting man."

"Where did you meet him?"

"It's hard *not* to meet men in this town." She slid into the driver's seat and started the motor.

"That's no answer."

"A woman is entitled to *some* secrets." She put the car into gear and drove away, leaving Hunter to stare after her with a frown on his face.

His concern was no consolation. It didn't offset his continued attempt to steer her toward Roger. She only hoped Hunter believed her story, instead of remembering that she was watching television on Friday night.

In spite of her personal problems, Bliss enjoyed her days at the studio. She fell into an easy relationship with the people on the set, and grew increasingly fond of

Melissa. The high point of her day, however, was the time spent with Hunter.

Bliss wanted to think she was the reason he visited the set so often, since his presence wasn't really required, but she was afraid to hope. Until she overheard two women talking. They didn't see her standing in the shadows.

"Do you have something lined up after this show?" a script girl named Margie asked.

"I'm working on Hunter Lord's next production, *Winter's End*," the other woman replied.

"Lucky you. I'd like to work with him—closely!"

"Don't get your hopes up. Bliss Goodwin has the inside track. Haven't you noticed the way he's always hanging around the set?"

"He's the producer," Margie pointed out.

"Since when do they come out of their ivory towers? No, I got the inside scoop from a secretary in Clay Dennison's office. The Lord has definitely got the hots for the missionary's daughter."

"Maybe that's what grabs him. Do you think I could score if I showed up in a Salvation Army uniform?"

"I don't know. It worked in *Guys and Dolls*." The laughter of the two women trailed back as they moved away.

Bliss was lit by an inner glow when she went home that afternoon. She joined Shelley on the patio, wearing a smile that told its own story.

"I gather the campaign to trap a Hunter is going well," Shelley remarked.

"How can you tell?"

"The last time I saw a smile like that was in a toothpaste ad."

"Things are looking up," Bliss admitted.

"Well, don't keep me in suspense. What did he say to you?"

"It wasn't anything he said, it was a conversation I overheard." Bliss's eyes sparkled with delight. "The rumor going around is that Hunter's crazy about me."

"I see." Shelley had obviously expected more.

"I know it's hard to believe. He hasn't exactly been monopolizing my time. But that's understandable. Hunter needs to work out some things in his own mind. There have been a couple of incidents between us that I'd rather not discuss."

"That's okay. I just hope everything works out for you."

"It will," Bliss lilted. "I'm on a roll."

She was even more confident the next day when Hunter brought her a gold bracelet with a heart-shaped charm. He *said* it was a token of gratitude for saving production costs.

"You've helped me often enough," she said shyly. "It's time I made a payment on the debt."

"You don't owe me anything, Bliss. If anything, it's the other way around." His voice deepened. "Since I've met you—" He didn't get to finish.

Mona appeared unexpectedly, her face white with strain. "I called your office and someone said you were here. Can I talk to you alone, Hunter?" She didn't even acknowledge Bliss.

After a look at Mona's tense expression, Hunter murmured to Bliss, "Excuse me for a moment. I'll be right back." They moved a short way off.

Bliss remained where Hunter left her, too dispirited to walk away. How could she have believed in her own importance? All Mona had to do was whistle and Hunter heeled.

At first Bliss was too wrapped up in her shattered dreams to hear their low-voiced conversation. Not that she wanted to. The portion that finally penetrated only made her more miserable.

"You shouldn't listen to rumor," Hunter was saying gently, his hands on Mona's shoulders. "You know how people like to gossip."

"I wish I could believe that's all it is," she answered tearfully.

"Come on, sweetheart. What man would cheat on a woman like you?"

Bliss finally summoned the energy to move, although her legs felt as leaden as her heart. She walked to the exit and out to her car.

Bliss wouldn't have gone to the studio the next day if it hadn't been for Melissa's lessons. Those were an obligation, but she left as soon as they were over. Until she mastered her crushing disappointment, seeing Hunter would be too painful.

She managed to avoid him for several days. When he didn't run into her on the set, Hunter called her at home, but Bliss had prepared for the possibility. She turned on the answering machine he'd bought her, and neglected to return his calls.

One day he finally tracked her down. Melissa had gone back to the set, and Bliss was putting away her books when Hunter appeared in the schoolroom.

"Where have you been?" he demanded. "And why didn't you return any of my phone calls?"

"I've been busy," she answered after the briefest glance at him.

"Too busy to dial a phone?"

"Yes."

"May I ask what's so important that you don't have time for anything else?"

"You wouldn't be interested." She closed the desk drawer and picked up her purse. "You'll have to excuse me now. I'm late for an appointment."

Hunter blocked her way. "What's wrong, Bliss? You've been avoiding me for days. Why?"

"You're imagining things. I told you, I'm busy. I...I met someone."

His eyes narrowed. "Does that mean you can't even talk to me?"

"Some other time. I really have to leave, Hunter."

He captured her chin in his palm, forcing her to look at him. "Not until you tell me what's bothering you— and don't say 'Nothing.' I know you better than that. What have I done to hurt your feelings?"

"I didn't think you credited me with having any," she said bitterly.

"Whatever I did was inadvertent, I assure you. Just tell me what it was so I can apologize."

His nearness was having a devastating effect. She twisted her chin away, unable to bear the contact with his hand a moment longer.

"It isn't important," she mumbled, turning her back.

"That's where you're wrong." His circling arms urged her around to face him. Gently stroking her pale hair he murmured, "Anything that upsets you is important to me."

Her common sense was being undermined by his deep velvet voice and potently masculine body. She wanted to believe everything he said and have him hold her close. The gift of joy was in his power.

She took a deep breath and forced the thought from her mind. But when she started to draw away he didn't release her.

"You'd better let me go, Hunter," she said tonelessly. "If anyone sees us it will start more rumors."

"People gossip whether they have cause or not."

"Mona might not be convinced a second time."

"What does she have to do with us?"

Bliss looked into his handsome face with outrage. Had his success with women confirmed his belief that he could manipulate all of them?

"I prefer the pitch you made to her. What man would look at another woman when he could have you, sweetheart?" she mimicked bitterly.

"You thought I was referring to myself?" he asked with dawning comprehension.

"Who else? You certainly pulled out all the stops to assure her! Not that it matters to me," she added belatedly. "Your love life is your own business."

"You've put a serious crimp in it," he said with a crooked smile.

"I'm sure you convinced Mona of your undying devotion. *I* was impressed."

When Bliss started for the door, Hunter stopped her effectively. He picked her up and sat her on the desk, keeping his hands at her waist. "You're going to sit here and listen while I explain what you think you heard. Mona is in love with Cullen Wainwright. They were talking about getting married, and then he landed the lead in a hit TV series. He's been out of town a lot, and she's afraid he's more than professionally interested in his very glamorous co-star. *Those* were the rumors I told her to ignore."

The steel band around Bliss's heart started to loosen, but she was afraid of being too gullible. "You were trying to get them back together?"

"I was advising her not to let vicious gossip spoil a beautiful relationship. I'd do the same for any good friend who wasn't thinking clearly."

"I feel foolish," Bliss murmured. "But anyone would have gotten the impression I got."

"Perhaps, but you didn't have to cut me out of your life."

"It seemed like the best thing to do if I was messing up yours. I didn't think you'd mind, anyway," she said in a small voice. "Sometimes you act as though you enjoy being with me, and then you seem to forget I'm alive."

"That would be an impossibility." His hands at her waist became almost unconsciously caressing. "I suppose my behavior must have seemed erratic, but that's because I've never been in a situation like this before. You know I'm attracted to you, Bliss, and you also know the problem. When I stay away from you I'm unhappy, and when I'm with you I'm tied up in knots."

"Have you ever considered that you might be in love?" Her laughter had a slight catch.

"I've tried not to," he said grimly.

Bliss knew at that moment that Hunter belonged to her. He was fighting the idea like a magnificent, unbroken stallion, but he would get used to the bridle if she didn't try to break him too fast.

"I was just diagnosing your symptoms, but I'm no authority," she said reassuringly. "Anyway, we can still be friends."

"I hope we always will be. I've missed seeing you this week," he murmured.

"I have an idea," she said artlessly. "Why don't you come for dinner tonight? I made a big pot of chili."

"That's one of my favorites."

"Really?" Her blue eyes widened. "What a lucky coincidence."

Hunter's behavior after their misunderstanding was thoroughly satisfactory. It was almost worth the misery Bliss had gone through. Instead of a brief few minutes on the set, he took her to dinner and to various events around town. On the weekends they played tennis or spent long lazy days around his pool.

A certain amount of sexual tension was always present between them, but Hunter did his best to defuse it. He made a concerted effort to avoid touching her except in the most casual way—an occasional arm around her shoulders, a hand outstretched to hoist her from the pool.

Bliss was secretly amused, but she let him set the pace. Once in a while she would slide her arm around his waist in the friendliest of fashions, and it delighted her to feel the tension in his lean body.

It was an idyllic period that couldn't last forever. One night Hunter told her they were ready to go on location.

"We leave on Monday, but you can still change your mind." He looked at her searchingly. "If you think it might be traumatic for you, don't hesitate to say so."

"You're not getting out of spending the night with me." When he gave her a startled glance, she added demurely, "Unless you want to call off the bet."

He recovered and began to chuckle. "Just start practicing your apology."

* * *

Bliss was filled with a mixture of emotions as she

stood at the railing of the yacht, searching the horizon for a glimpse of her island. One of the most surprising emotions was anticipation. The months on the tiny atoll had been filled with loneliness and deprivation certainly, but every minute hadn't been bad. She had a proprietary feeling toward the place that had sheltered her.

Hunter appeared beside her at the railing. "The captain says we're almost there." He scanned the limitless expanse of blue water, shaking his head. "It must be a mere dot in the ocean. I don't know how he can find such a tiny target in an area this vast."

"It looked huge to me when I washed up on the beach."

"I can imagine." He put his arm around her and hugged her tightly.

Bliss rested her head contentedly on Hunter's shoulder, watching flying fish glitter in the sunshine before plunging back into the sea. It was the kind of blue-and-gold day she remembered.

"I hope this weather holds," Hunter remarked. "We were warned that fierce storms can spring up out of nowhere."

"Believe it!" she said with feeling. "The studio crew will be in for a big surprise if one hits. They think they're going to Waikiki Beach."

"Wait till they try unloading heavy equipment from a rocking motorboat. They'll start earning their keep."

So far the trip had been like a deluxe vacation. They'd flown first class to the coast of Africa where they boarded a sleek yacht. The accommodations were luxurious, and a party mood prevailed.

Mona joined them on deck. "I hear we're about half an hour away."

She looked like someone out of a travel brochure, the kind of tourist every woman dreamed of being. Her figure-hugging white pants and navy blazer were wrinkle free, and the breeze ruffled her long blond hair becomingly. Flawless skin and perfect teeth completed a picture of unattainable perfection.

Bliss wondered again how Hunter could possibly feel only friendship for this woman, but she was convinced that was the case. He and Mona had a warm, caring relationship without any desire being present.

The visual proof gratified Bliss, while making her faintly uneasy at the same time. Hunter had been in love with Mona once, or at least they'd had a relationship. If his heart hadn't been involved then, what made her think this time was any different? Would he feel only friendship for *her* one day?

She refused to let the possibility discourage her. Everything about their situation was different. Sooner or later Hunter would have to admit it to himself and give in.

The island appeared first as a slight smudge separating sea and sky. It gained form and color as they approached, but retained the illusion of a mirage. One small speck of land was incongruous in the middle of the ocean.

As they drew nearer, a strip of white sand was visible with lush green growth in the background. Tall palm trees waved languidly, and an occasional bird soared through the air, the only sign of life in a primeval paradise.

Mona stared in fascination. "Nothing you told us prepared me for this. I had no idea it was such a small island."

"Wait till we get closer. It's larger than it looks from here," Bliss said. "I'll give you a tour, but you'd better change into something more rugged. The trails I cut are bound to be overgrown by now."

By the time the yacht dropped anchor everybody was lining the railing, impatient to go ashore for a better look. They crowded onto the launch, making excited comments.

Bliss left the others at the water's edge and walked slowly up the beach. Parting the verdant foliage that bordered the sand, she stepped back into the past. Everything was just as she remembered it. The walls of her rude shelter sagged in places, and the clearing in front was covered with debris, but nothing was greatly changed.

The ship's hatch table reminded her of the solitary meals she'd eaten there, making comments aloud to hear the sound of her own voice. Inside the hut were the minor treasures she'd rescued from the sea, neatly stored in coconut shells and plastic containers. It was as though the island was waiting to reclaim her.

Unreasoning panic closed Bliss's throat. What if everyone returned to the ship and left her here? She turned and started to run back to the beach.

Hunter stood at the edge of the clearing. He had followed at a distance, not wanting to intrude. When he saw the look on her face he opened his arms.

"It's all right, darling," he soothed, gathering her trembling body close. "Nothing can hurt you now."

She tightened her arms around his waist. "I was afraid you'd leave me."

"Don't ever think such a thing." He kissed the top of her head. "I'll always be here if you need me."

The sound of voices on the beach made Bliss realize she'd been a victim of nerves. "I don't know what came over me," she murmured, her fears vanishing in the safety of his embrace.

"I was worried that you might be affected like this. Do you want to go back to the ship?" he asked gravely.

"No, I'm fine now." She drew away reluctantly.

Hunter squeezed her hand reassuringly as the others came noisily through the underbrush. Their presence brought a sense of reality.

"This is a real bonus," Rafe exclaimed, catching sight of the hut. "With a little fixing up we can use that shack instead of building a new one."

"The lighting won't be easy," Fred, the head camera-man, remarked.

"Easy is being a shoe salesman," Rafe answered dismissively. "Get Cassie over here. I want her to start making a list of what we'll need."

The previously quiet spot was soon swarming with people, the loud voices chasing away ghosts.

Mona had followed Bliss's instructions and changed into jeans and tennis shoes. "Okay, I'm ready for the grand tour. But if you're only going to show me more palm trees, I'd just as soon go for a swim."

"Be adventurous. Are you coming, Hunter?"

"Right behind you," he said.

Bliss led the way through a tropical wilderness that looked as though it hadn't been disturbed since the beginning of time. It took her experienced eyes to find the trail that had once been there. Without hesitation she plunged into the lush greenery.

"You didn't tell us we had to fight our way through a jungle," Mona grumbled. "Where are we going?"

"It's only a little farther," Bliss assured her.

A short time later they came out of the tangled vegetation to a spot of such surpassing beauty that Mona forgot her complaint. A clearing was surrounded by tall trees. In the middle was a pond fed by a waterfall that cascaded down a hill. The murmuring water danced over rocks and lichen before subsiding into a deep blue pool studded with water lilies.

"I've never seen anything so gorgeous." Mona gasped. "I'd like to jump in right this minute."

"The water isn't as warm as the ocean," Bliss warned. "It comes from hidden springs."

"I don't care. You won't have to double for me in the scenes we shoot here. I'm going to do these myself."

"Be my guest. Just don't be startled if you have company." Bliss grinned.

"Not something disgusting like eels, I hope." Mona cast a less sanguine glance at the picturesque pool.

"Nothing that bad, depending on your viewpoint. This spot is the playground for frogs as big as footballs."

"You're kidding!"

"That's just Bliss's little joke," Hunter said.

"You won't find out unless you spend the night here. Want to forfeit the bet?" she taunted.

"On the contrary. I'm looking forward to it," he answered. "Under the same conditions you did."

"You two are actually going to sleep on the ground when there's a yacht within shouting distance?" Mona asked incredulously.

"Unless Bliss admits she was exaggerating. To show what an understanding fellow I am, you don't even have to apologize," he told Bliss. "Simply admit you were putting me on."

She smiled enchantingly. "I'm not nearly as nice a person as you are. I want my written apology."

"Okay, if you want to carry a joke to extremes. But I warn you, I won't let you forget I won."

"We'll see, won't we?" she murmured.

Chapter Ten

The bet between Bliss and Hunter was the talk of the ship during dinner. Opinion was divided on whether she was setting him up or not.

"Any of you are welcome to join us," Bliss said. "It should be lots of fun. Sometimes a brief shower passes over toward morning, but you'll dry off when the sun comes up."

"Pure scare tactics," Hunter scoffed. "She'll do anything to win a bet. How many of you want to come with us?"

It turned out that nobody did. Rafe declined on the grounds that he couldn't afford to catch cold, and the others had various excuses.

"I can rough it at home, but how often do I get to live it up on a yacht?" Fred asked, which seemed to sum up the general feeling.

Bliss and Hunter were given a joking send-off as they climbed down a rope ladder into the motor launch. The ship was gaily lit and the moon silvered a path of light over the water. In contrast, the dark island looked faintly forbidding.

"We'll see you in the morning if you survive an attack by the giant frogs," Rafe called.

"I hope the frogs are the only ones that croak," one of the others joked.

"None of you would make it as stand-up comics," Mona told them disgustedly. She leaned over the railing with a worried expression. "Won't you at least take a flashlight?"

Hunter waved to her from the motorboat. "Don't worry, I'm in Bliss's capable hands. See you in the morning."

It was pitch-black in the dense thicket, and Bliss had trouble finding the faint trail. She began to wish they'd taken Mona's advice about the flashlight. Trailing creepers caught in her hair like clutching fingers, and she had to backtrack a couple of times when barriers of palmetto proved impenetrable.

"I don't remember all these obstacles. Is this an added trial to test my endurance?" Hunter asked suspiciously.

"It just seems longer in the dark," she answered, not wanting him to guess they were lost.

Before she had to admit it, the sound of splashing water guided her to the clearing. It was like emerging into a miniature Eden. The lovely spot was even more magical at night with spray from the waterfall glittering like diamonds in the moonlight.

"This must have made up a little bit for your ordeal," Hunter said in a hushed voice.

"Except that I wanted someone to share it with."

His hand reached out for hers and held on tightly. But when she looked up at him with luminous eyes he remarked with forced heartiness, "All right, we're here. Where are the frogs?"

"They aren't pets. I can't whistle for them."

"I'm beginning to think this was all a hoax to get me here. To see if I could take it, I mean," he added hastily.

Before she could answer there was a loud plop in the pool, followed by another. She pointed over his shoulder excitedly. "Now do you believe me?"

"I didn't see anything."

"Well, you heard it. Will you admit a splash that loud had to be made by something huge?"

"How about a coconut?"

"Sit down and be quiet," she ordered.

They sat cross-legged by the pool, straining their eyes toward the widening ripples in the water. For long moments the only other motion came from leaves stirred by the breeze.

Suddenly a humongous frog leaped out of the bushes and landed on a lily pad. He remained fixed for a moment, then his throat swelled and he uttered a resounding croak. It was answered by a chorus of other croaks, and soon the lily pads were alive with green, bulging-eyed monsters.

"I wouldn't have believed it," Hunter breathed.

"I know. It was a revelation to me, too, the first time," Bliss said magnanimously. "Don't tell anybody else about them, though."

"You already did. That's why we're here."

"Only so *you* could see them. I planned to tell the others it was a joke."

"That wouldn't be very wise. They might get the wrong idea."

"About our wanting to spend the night together?" Her eyes held his.

"Yes." He stood abruptly. "Now that you've won the bet we might as well go back to the ship. It's pointless to stay here all night."

"I suppose you're right."

Bliss rested her forehead on her raised knees. If Hunter didn't succumb to the romance of this idyllic spot, he was totally immune. You couldn't make someone fall in love with you, she was finding out the hard way.

"Bliss, honey." Hunter knelt on one knee beside her. "Don't make this more difficult for me."

She raised her head. "It's all right. I understand."

"I'm not sure you do." He looked at her searchingly.

"I didn't before, but I do now. I've been trying to read something into our relationship that isn't there."

"You know I'm very fond of you," he said hesitantly.

"Don't, Hunter!" Her voice was sharp. "I'm not a child. I can take rejection without having a tantrum."

He sighed. "You're determined to misunderstand."

"You're the one who isn't being straightforward. Why can't you admit you're not interested in me romantically?"

A nerve throbbed in his temple. "If you only knew how much I want to make love to you."

"Then what's stopping you? This isn't like the other times. You aren't seducing me, and I haven't had too much to drink."

"If I was sure you knew what you were doing," he muttered. "That you wouldn't hate me afterward."

Bliss sat perfectly still. She knew his tight control would snap if she made the first move, but that wasn't the way she wanted him. Neither of them must have any regrets afterward.

"You mean so much to me." He reached out and touched her cheek gently. "I couldn't stand it if you went out of my life because I took advantage of your generosity."

"I love you, Hunter," she said softly. "I would never leave you."

He stared at her almost harshly. "If I could only believe that."

"Can't you tell?" she whispered.

His expression changed as he gathered her in his arms and reached for her mouth. His kiss was almost bruising in its fierce intensity, but Bliss didn't mind. She felt the same need to possess and be possessed. Digging her fingers into his shoulders, she pulled him off balance. They toppled full length onto the velvety grass, their bodies pressed together.

Finally Hunter dragged his mouth away and buried his face in her throat. "I thought this moment would never come."

"I did, too." She pulled the T-shirt out of his jeans and kneaded the lithe muscles rippling under his smooth skin. "I'd almost given up hope that it would ever happen. Tell me you won't leave me this time."

"I couldn't if I tried," he murmured, bending his head to kiss the taut peaks that strained against the fabric of her blouse. "How could I give up such loveliness?"

A streak of liquid fire raced through her veins as he unbuttoned her blouse, then removed it along with her bra. The cool night air couldn't quench the flames he lit when he caressed her naked breasts.

"Your body is utter perfection," he said in a husky voice. "I love to look at you and touch you. I want to be part of you."

"That's what I've dreamed about night after night," she whispered.

Pushing his T-shirt under his arms, Bliss pulled him against her. She needed to feel the contact of their bare bodies, with no barrier to blunt the exquisite sensation.

"I'll make up for every wasted hour," he promised as he stripped off his shirt, then clasped her in his arms again. "I want it to be so wonderful for you, sweetheart."

"It already is," she gasped.

"My little angel." His mouth covered hers, escalating her passion.

It mounted even higher when Hunter unzipped her jeans and slid them down her hips. The pair of sheer panties that were her only remaining garment soon followed, and then she was completely nude. In the silvery moonlight her skin gleamed like a pearl. Hunter's eyes were incandescent as he stared down at her, stroking her thighs with maddening deliberation.

"Please, darling." She gasped. "I want you so."

"Soon, my love."

He parted her legs gently and lowered his head to kiss the soft white skin of her inner thigh. Shock waves traveled through her entire body as his scorching mouth continued its devastation. She reached for him blindly, murmuring his name over and over.

Hunter's restraint vanished when he gazed at her rapturous face. Flinging off the rest of his clothes in a blur of motion, he returned to cover her body with his.

She stiffened once, but he held her tenderly. "Let it happen, darling," he said gently.

She relaxed in the embrace of the man she loved and trusted. Soon the flickering flames flared up anew and she moved against him, tentatively at first, then with growing assurance. Her body grew taut as Hunter drove her to the outer limits of endurance. Waves of pleasure washed over her, growing in intensity until she reached the highest peak and cried out in ecstasy.

The descent was gradual. Fulfillment took the place of urgency as she spiraled back to earth, her body still throbbing with satisfaction.

Hunter was looking at her gravely when her eyelashes finally fluttered open. "Was it all you expected?"

She smiled enchantingly. "And so much more."

"I'm glad." He kissed her with infinite sweetness.

"You didn't get to be such a fabulous lover without knowing it would be."

"How would you know if I'm good or not?" he teased.

"Nobody could be any better."

"I'm going to see to it that you never have a chance to make comparisons." He chuckled.

Bliss held her breath. Was Hunter about to propose?

He reached for her blouse, instead. "Are you warm enough? I don't want you to catch cold."

"I'm glowing all over," she assured him.

He kissed her with warm affection, and for a time they were content to lie quietly under the stars. The night sounds all around provided exotic background music.

"Why don't you want the others to know about the frogs?" Hunter finally asked languidly.

"I'm sorry I ever mentioned them. This is their home, where they've lived for who knows how many hundreds of years. If word got around, someone would want to bring back specimens. They'd be put under a microscope and treated like freaks, just because they're different.''

"I understand," he said gently.

Her serious mood was replaced by a captivating smile. "Maybe frogs fall in love and get married like anyone else. I wouldn't want to be responsible for breaking up happy families, would you?''

"The way I feel right now, I'd like to be godfather to their children." His eyes started to glow as he wound his legs around hers.

It was a night of passion that Bliss couldn't have imagined in her most wishful fantasies. Hunter initiated her into all the mysteries of love, transporting her to heights she'd never reached. They fell asleep twined together, and awoke with renewed ardor, as though discovering each other for the first time.

Rays of light filtering through the tall trees wakened them before the sun came up. Hunter opened his eyes to find Bliss gazing at him with wonder.

"I thought you were only a dream," she said softly.

"Do you often have dreams that vivid?" he teased.

"Ever since I met you."

"Dear little Bliss."

She slipped out of his arms as they started to tighten around her. "We'd better get dressed. The others will be along soon."

"Not this early. They all think they're on a vacation, an impression I intend to correct speedily."

"You weren't worrying about production costs last night," she said mischievously.

"I was keeping the star happy. At least I hope I was."

She leaned forward and kissed the hollow in his throat. "You can't have any doubt about that."

"I haven't exhausted the possibilities yet," he murmured.

Bliss laughed. "A cold shower might change your mind." Before he could stop her, she jumped up and ran to the waterfall.

Hunter followed and plunged in after her, unsuspecting. His howls of outrage sent birds flying out of the trees.

"Why didn't you tell me the water was freezing?" He gasped.

"You'll warm up after a few laps around the pool."

Her body sliced through the calm surface, churning up the water as she swam briskly. Hunter followed her advice and soon caught up with her. They swam side by side until the vigorous activity warmed their blood.

"Wasn't that refreshing?" Bliss asked when she finally sank down on some submerged rocks near the edge of the pond.

"After the first shock, which could have killed me. You delight in surprising me."

"Isn't that the way to keep a man interested?"

"You don't have to resort to trickery. I was hooked from the minute I walked into your hotel room that first day."

"You took long enough to show it," she complained.

"I was enjoying having you chase me." He chuckled.

"Of all the male chauvinist arrogance!" Moving swiftly, she pushed him off the rock. Hunter was caught unawares, and his head disappeared beneath the surface. He reappeared with a determined gleam in his eyes.

"So you want to play games."

"You deserved that," she told him while prudently starting to scramble for the bank.

One hand caught her by the ankle, then an arm hooked around her waist and tumbled her back into the water.

"Let me go, Hunter," she squealed. "We don't have time to fool around."

"You should have thought of that before you started to fling insults about. A little dose of your own medicine is called for."

As he tilted her backward, Bliss clasped her arms around his neck and clung tightly. Between peals of laughter she said, "Okay, you win. I forced you to make love to me. Does that satisfy you?"

He bent over her, supporting her head just above the water. As her hair streamed out in a fan of floating tendrils, Hunter touched his lips gently to hers.

"You satisfy me in every way possible," he murmured deeply.

Her laughter died. "Do you really mean that, Hunter? I was worried that..."

Her voice trailed off as she looked at him searchingly. It had been wonderful for her, but Bliss knew she lacked the experience of other women he'd known. Could she really be enough for him?

"How can you even ask?"

"Because I couldn't bear to lose you," she answered simply. "Not now."

His expression altered as he stared down at her yearning face. "I hope you'll always feel this way," he muttered. "I fought a losing battle, but you're mine now. I'll never let you go."

"Why would I want to?" She smoothed the deep furrow between his eyebrows.

Hunter's face softened as he kissed her fingertips. "You're right, my love. I'm just borrowing trouble. We'll make it work."

Bliss didn't know what he was worried about, but when his mouth sought her breast and warmed each coral rosette with his tongue, nothing else seemed important.

His hands skimmed her body tantalizingly, lingering at each vulnerable spot until she moaned with pleasure. The lapping water was an extension of his caresses, flowing sensuously over her skin.

When she reached out to touch him with the same intimacy, he uttered a hoarse cry that was as basic as the elements surrounding them. In the golden light of the rising sun, rocked by the subtly erotic motion of the water, Hunter took deep possession.

Their passion seemed unquenchable. They moved against each other with a primitive need that was timeless. Bliss met his driving force with a response that quickened his already frenzied motions. The tension ended in a burst of power that brought release to their straining bodies.

Hunter held her tightly while their heartbeats returned to normal. "I can't seem to get enough of you," he murmured.

She stroked his hair slowly. "You'll have plenty of time. I'm not going anywhere."

He stirred reluctantly. "I wish we didn't have to move from this spot, but we'll have company soon."

"How could I have forgotten?" she exclaimed, suddenly energized.

"Because you have your priorities in the right place." He grinned.

Bliss and Hunter were dressed and waiting on the beach when the launch approached. They were greeted with a barrage of joking remarks.

"I see you lived to talk about it," Rafe called. "How were the monster frogs?"

"We had a bet on that you'd chicken out," Fred said as they all climbed out and milled around.

"I was rooting for you, though," Cassie, the production assistant, said.

"Sure, because you had a bundle riding on him," Rafe complained. "I figured nobody with a grain of sense would camp out without even a sleeping bag."

"It was an experience," Hunter said lightly.

"So is skydiving, but I wouldn't want to do that, either."

"Did you at least see the frogs?" Mona asked.

"No, they must have been vacationing on another island," Hunter answered.

"So you were a loser, too," Rafe said to Bliss.

"I wouldn't say that," she remarked demurely. "As Hunter said, it was an experience."

"Oh, really?" Rafe regarded them speculatively.

"I realize you're all fascinated by our adventure, but might I suggest we get down to work?" Hunter asked.

The days that followed were packed with activity. Everyone rose early and worked late. No matter what time they returned to the ship, however, a sumptuous meal awaited them.

After dinner some of the crew played cards in the grand salon, while others relaxed on lounge chairs under the stars, or strolled around the deck. Bliss and Hunter drifted from one group to another for a while, then discreetly went down to her cabin.

They made love without urgency, discovering every secret thing about each other, delighting in finding new ways to give pleasure. When their passion was spent they remained joined together in shared satisfaction.

It was an idyllic time except for one thing. Hunter always insisted on going back to his own cabin sometime before dawn. Bliss couldn't change his mind with either arguments or pleading, although she continued to try. It was an ongoing disagreement between them—the only one.

"Nobody would think anything of it if we spent the night together," she pointed out fruitlessly. "Especially in this business."

"That's just the point. You're not like other people in this business," Hunter continued to state firmly.

"I presume it's my reputation you're worried about, but if I'm not concerned, why should you be?"

"Everything about you is important to me," he said tenderly.

Bliss always melted at that throbbing note in his voice, and they usually made love once more before he left.

She realized why Hunter considered it important to pretend they weren't involved. Morals were fairly relaxed among the production crew. Bliss knew of several attachments that had been formed on this trip, casual affairs owing more to opportunity and sex drive than to any real feeling for one another. The affairs would end amicably when they returned home. Both partners accepted the fact. Bliss sensed that Hunter didn't want their own relationship viewed in that light.

She longed to suggest an alternative—becoming engaged—but she was afraid of rushing him. Hunter was so vehemently opposed to Hollywood marriages. He needed time to get used to the idea that theirs would be different.

Outside of that one stumbling block, life couldn't have been more perfect. Even the weather cooperated. The days continued to be sunny and the nights clear, with no rain to hold up production. They were scheduled to shoot a night scene at the waterfall when Mona approached Bliss tentatively.

"Now that I've seen how you lived here, I realize I made some dumb suggestions when we first met."

Bliss had almost forgotten her prejudice against the other woman. "That's okay. I was a little inflexible at the time."

"How much have you loosened up?"

"Why?" Bliss asked warily.

"You were annoyed when I saw this part as an opportunity to look glamorous, and you were perfectly right," Mona said earnestly. "But when we shoot at the waterfall tonight, could I wear just one water lily in my hair? Didn't you ever feel like doing that just for your own sake? It's such a romantic spot."

"It is when you're with someone," Bliss answered softly.

"Even documentaries take a few liberties. It wouldn't be out of character," Mona insisted.

Bliss smiled. "You can wear a whole crown of water lilies with my blessing."

"You *have* mellowed." Mona slanted a glance at her. "This wouldn't have anything to do with the night you camped out with Hunter, would it?"

Bliss didn't have to answer. Her pink cheeks gave her away.

"I thought there was something going on between you two."

"I hope that doesn't disturb you." Bliss was suddenly apprehensive. "I mean, I heard you and Hunter— In fact, at one time I thought maybe you still—"

"Hunter and I had a great relationship, but we both knew we weren't right for each other. For one thing, we're too much alike. I'm competitive and demanding just like he is. We've remained friends though, and I'm proud of that. Hunter is tops in my book. He's one of the few people you'll meet who has real integrity. Hang on to him."

"I'm certainly going to try."

Hunter joined them with a querying look. "What's going on?"

Mona grinned. "Bliss and I were comparing notes."

He was suddenly wary. "I don't think I want to know the subject."

"Relax, darling. Neither of us would say anything bad about you." Mona blew him a kiss before departing.

Hunter searched Bliss's face. "What has Mona been telling you?"

"We had an interesting conversation."

"I've never lied to you, Bliss. I told you Mona and I had a relationship that ended years ago. I can't believe she told you differently."

"She didn't," Bliss soothed. "That's one nice lady. She told me how lucky I am, and I agree."

"You told Mona about us?"

"I didn't have to. She guessed. You don't mind, do you?" Bliss asked uncertainly.

"I suppose not. As long as she doesn't tell the whole crew. I'll have a talk with her."

"Hunter, we're having a problem over here," Rafe called.

Bliss remained where he left her, trying to ignore the demons of doubt that cast a shadow over her newfound happiness. She hadn't imagined Hunter's displeasure at having their feelings become known. Was he really protecting the reputation of a missionary's daughter, or was his reason more personal? If he intended this as a brief interlude that would end when the documentary did, it would be easier to avoid gossip if nobody knew.

That night after dinner she pleaded a headache and went down to her cabin alone. When Hunter knocked softly at the door a little later, she pretended to be asleep.

Through the long night Bliss was torn by indecision. She was so inexperienced; Hunter could deceive her easily. But nobody could fake the passion he'd displayed. That part could be genuine, though. Men didn't need to be in love to enjoy sex. And yet . . . could she really be that bad a judge of character? By morning Bliss hadn't decided.

Hunter was very solicitous at breakfast. "How do you feel, honey? You look a little rocky. Maybe you'd better stay aboard ship today."

"I feel fine," she answered shortly. "I can't goof off, anyway. I'm scheduled to double for Mona in the ocean scene."

"We can put it off until tomorrow."

"That won't be necessary. The exercise will do me good." She pushed back her chair and left the table before he could stop her.

They didn't get around to her scene until almost noon. "Okay, Bliss," Rafe finally called. "Take off your clothes and hand them to Cassie. We'll wait until you're in the water to start rolling."

Before she could voice an objection, Hunter erupted. "Are you crazy? She's not going to swim in the nude!"

"What do you expect her to wear?" Rafe asked. "She didn't have a bathing suit."

"Focus on her head and shoulders."

"Part of her body might show. What's the big deal? In a long shot nothing will be really clear."

"No," Hunter stated firmly. "You can't ask her to do that. It isn't in her contract."

"Why don't we let her decide? Bliss, do you—"

"Don't try to pressure her," Hunter ordered before Rafe could finish. "She's not going to do it."

"Be reasonable, Hunter. We've established the fact that she swam naked all those months. Mona's nude scene in the pool was tastefully done. Why are you throwing up roadblocks all of a sudden?"

"Mona is a professional actress who knew what she was signing on for," Hunter answered in clipped tones. "Bliss intends to be a teacher. How do you think a school board would feel about hiring an already celebrated person who appeared nude on camera?"

The hard core of happiness in Bliss's chest dissolved in a rush of love. Hunter's only thought all along had been to protect her. As the argument raged between the two men, she stood there smiling.

They eventually resolved the dispute by sending the motorboat back to the ship for a flesh-colored bodysuit of Mona's.

Bliss was too ashamed to admit her earlier suspicions, but that night in her stateroom she was even more passionate than usual.

Hunter was a little overwhelmed. "You must really have missed me last night," he commented.

"This has been such a heavenly time," she answered indirectly. "I never thought I'd say it, but I don't want to leave the island. I'll miss being with you every night."

"It isn't like we won't see each other again." He fit her body closer to his. "You don't think I'd let you get away now, do you?"

"It won't be the same as being together constantly the way we have been."

"Maybe that's all for the best." He smiled. "I don't want you to get tired of me."

She trailed her fingers over the hard plane of his hip, down a muscular flank lightly roughened by crisp hair. The perfection of Hunter's body never failed to amaze her.

"How could I ever tire of the man I love?" she asked softly. "You taught me to be a woman in the fullest sense."

Strangely enough, the compliment didn't please him. "I'm glad your initiation was a good experience, but confusing gratification with love is very common, especially the first time."

"How can you say that?" she asked in a hurt voice.

"Because it's true," he answered harshly.

"You don't want me to be in love with you, do you, Hunter?"

Bliss suddenly realized he had never declared his own feelings. Hunter had flattered her with many extravagant and arousing words—but never the ones she wanted to hear.

"I wish I was convinced that you know what love is." His eyes were somber.

"I know that I've never cared about anyone like this before. I also know that love is more than just sex. But maybe it isn't for you." She drew away from him and pulled the sheet up to cover her nakedness. "You're the one who will lose interest, not I."

"If you only knew how wrong you are." His deep voice vibrated with feeling. "I'm tormented by the thought of losing you. That's why I fought against getting too deeply involved."

"You said that before, but I didn't believe you were serious." She stared at him incredulously. "You're the legend. The man who could have any woman he wanted."

"I've never wanted anyone this much. I love you, Bliss." His voice was filled with wonder.

Her heart swelled until she thought it might burst. The prayerfully hoped for had finally happened. Her wild stallion was tamed at last.

"Come back to me," he murmured, pulling down the sheet.

Hunter's lovemaking was intense, as though he was determined to commit himself fully. His hot mouth scorched her skin, and his hands and body tantalized her almost beyond endurance. She flamed in his arms and begged for more, until the final embrace set them both free.

Bliss was asleep when Hunter eased cautiously out of bed. She frowned and reached for him, but didn't waken. Moonlight coming through the porthole etched her delicate features and turned her hair to spun silver.

He stood perfectly still staring down at her, his eyes hooded. "Innocent little Bliss. I'll be glad when this is over. Would you understand why I didn't tell you everything?"

Los Angeles seemed especially hectic after the peace and quiet of the tropics. The studio had sent a car and driver to pick them up, but being in a limo didn't make the traffic any less abominable. Bliss winced as horns blared all around them. She breathed a sigh of relief when the car turned onto her quiet street.

Hunter carried her luggage into the apartment and kissed her briefly. "Get some rest, honey."

"Aren't you going to stay?" she asked, disappointed.

"I can't. I have to phone the studio and see what's been happening while I've been away. There are probably a million things that need my attention."

"Surely they can wait until tomorrow."

"Not really. Besides, the car is waiting."

"You could tell him you don't need him anymore."

"I have to go home. Do you want me to get in trouble with Max?" Hunter chuckled. "He hasn't had anybody to yell at in almost two weeks. I'll talk to you later, angel."

Bliss stared after him with fond annoyance. His priorities left a lot to be desired, but she'd just have to be patient. Hunter could be led, but not driven, she was finding out.

Chapter Eleven

Bliss was unpacking when Shelley dropped by. "I saw your lights so I knew you were back. How was your trip?"

"Fantastic!"

"That's great. Tell me all about it."

After Bliss had described the island and what it was like to live on a yacht and be waited on royally, Shelley said, "Now for the good part. Did you and Mona scratch each other's eyes out over Hunter? And if so, who won?"

"It wasn't like that at all. Mona's truly in love with someone else. She couldn't have been nicer to me."

"How about Hunter? Was he nice to you, too?"

"I think you could safely say that." Bliss's breathless laughter and pink cheeks told the story.

"I'm really happy for you. He's an awesome hunk of man."

"I know," Bliss said softly.

Shelley chuckled. "I'm sure you do."

"I didn't mean only that," Bliss protested. "He's wonderful in every way. You wouldn't believe some of the things he said to me."

"You'd better not, either. The best of them can't be trusted. Just enjoy."

"You're such a cynic! I'll remind you of those words at my wedding."

Shelley gave her a surprised look. "Hunter proposed?"

"Well, not yet, but he will. He told me he loved me."

"And you think—" Shelley checked her impulsive reaction. "The last thing I want to do is let the air out of your balloon. But just because a guy tells you he loves you while he's—well, let's just say he isn't thinking about a rose-covered cottage at that point."

"You simply don't understand," Bliss said impatiently. "This isn't a casual affair. We care deeply about each other. The only reason he hasn't proposed already is because he wants *me* to be sure."

"That's a new angle."

"You're impossible!" Bliss exclaimed.

"I'm only warning you not to expect miracles. What you have now isn't so bad."

Bliss sighed happily. "That's the first time I ever heard heaven described so casually." She changed the subject, not wanting to argue any longer. "How are you and Kirk doing?"

"Okay. He got a bit part in a movie, so at least I don't have to support him this month. All I have to worry about are the extras who won't leave him alone." Shelley's light tone indicated it was a joke.

Bliss wasn't fooled, but she pretended to be joking, too. "You could teach him to say the word no. It only has one syllable."

"I was never good at living in a dreamworld." Shelley gave her a twisted smile and stood up. "Well, I'd better go to work."

Max called Bliss the next morning. "Welcome back. Did you have a good time?"

"I had a wonderful time!"

"That's good. What did you do to the boss? He's almost human."

Bliss laughed. "You sound disappointed. What's the matter? Do you miss your sparring partner?"

"In a way. It's a little scary to see a tiger turn into a house cat."

"Give him some of your good advice, he'll get his roar back."

"I've decided to enjoy the calm while it lasts. How would you like to come over for dinner tonight and see us get along for a change?"

"It would be an experience to cherish. Can I help? I don't have anything to do today."

"Come over for a swim, then."

Bliss was a little miffed that Hunter hadn't phoned her, but she realized he must be swamped with work after being away so long. He probably wouldn't even make it home for dinner until late, but at least they'd have the night together.

Driving up to Hunter's house was like coming home, and Max's genuine pleasure at seeing her heightened the feeling. They sat around the pool talking like old friends. Bliss told him how well the crew liked Hunter, and how he'd kept everything running smoothly.

"He's a genius, all right." Max changed the subject casually. "How did you get along with Mona?"

"Just great. She's a real trouper. I was impressed with the way she did the nude scenes. They didn't faze her a bit."

"She doesn't have anything to be ashamed of," Max remarked dryly.

"I know." Bliss looked suddenly wistful. "Mona makes the average woman look like a boy."

"What do you care? You're not average."

She smiled. "That's a nice compliment, Max."

"I used to turn a nifty phrase in my day. I've been around, kid."

"What did you do before you came to work for Hunter? He told me he doesn't know anything about you."

"He knows all he needs to. The boss and I don't mess in each other's affairs."

Bliss's eyes danced with merriment. "I'll bet he'd dispute that."

"Well, sometimes I have to straighten him out," Max conceded. "But it's always for his own good."

"What if he doesn't agree?"

"That's not news. We never agree."

"Even in the beginning?"

He shrugged. "Who can remember back that far?"

She grinned. "You must have some funny memories of those early days when you were getting used to each other."

"I don't think about the past," he said curtly.

Bliss was surprised. Max was always a little abrupt, that was just his way, but this time he sounded almost surly. What nerve had she touched?

He glanced over at her sober face. "I'm sorry. I didn't need to bite your head off."

"It's all right, I should have known better. I don't like it, either, when people pry into my past."

He stared at her silently, as though making up his mind. "Maybe I shouldn't have buried it so deep. The headshrinkers say it screws you all up. But in the beginning it was too painful to think about, then after a while it was like a story I once heard about someone else."

"You don't have to explain," she said gently.

"For the first time I feel like telling somebody," he mused, scarcely hearing her comment. "Maybe that's a good sign." With his eyes on the distant trees, Max said, "I grew up in an orphanage back east. Never knew my parents, or if I had any brothers or sisters. They didn't mistreat me there or anything like that, but from the beginning I knew nothing was going to be handed to me.

"When I got out of school I scraped up enough money to buy a beat-up van. I fixed it up as a canteen, and went around to the colleges peddling snacks and cold drinks. Built up a regular clientele. One of my steady customers was a beautiful blond girl named Dawn. Isn't that a pretty name?"

"Very pretty," Bliss murmured, although she had a feeling he was talking to himself.

"She was always very friendly, but I didn't take it personally. What would a girl like that want with a guy like me? Dawn was the one who finally asked *me* for a date. We fell in love so fast I couldn't believe it." His reminiscent smile faded. "Her parents didn't, either. They threatened to pull her out of school if she didn't stop seeing me. We couldn't change their minds, so we decided to elope."

He paused for so long that Bliss said, "Did her parents find out and stop you?"

"No, everything went according to plan." His voice was suddenly lifeless. "Dawn smuggled a suitcase out and drove her car to my rooming house. Only she never got there. Some drunken bum driving too fast skidded on the ice and plowed into her. She never knew what hit her."

"Oh, Max, how tragic!"

"Yeah. She was the love of my life. Nobody could ever take her place."

"I'm so sorry," Bliss said helplessly.

He appeared to notice her for the first time. "That's why it burns me to see couples who are right for each other wasting precious time because they're too dumb to do anything about it."

"Maybe they aren't always as dumb as you think," she said softly.

He regarded her with satisfaction. "I wouldn't mind being wrong once in a while."

They didn't refer to Max's past again, but the fact that he'd told her about it formed a bond between them. They spent a pleasant afternoon talking idly, and Max even allowed her to help him in the kitchen.

Hunter didn't get home until late, as Bliss surmised. He looked tired, but his face lit up when he saw her. "What a lovely surprise."

"I was hoping you'd think so."

"Does this convince you?" He took her in his arms and kissed her.

After a satisfactory time she drew back and traced the faint lines on his forehead. "Did you have a hard day?"

"It was pretty hectic. Budget reports and phone calls all morning, and meetings all afternoon. I didn't get to view the rushes until five o'clock."

"Poor baby. Take off your tie and be comfortable. Max and I prepared all your favorites for dinner."

"What's he softening me up for? A raise?"

"Stop picking on poor Max. I helped. Do you suspect me of ulterior motives, also?"

Hunter chuckled. "I already know what *you* want."

"Of all the conceited males!" she exclaimed indignantly.

"Not conceited, grateful." He pulled her close and blew softly in her ear. "I'm glad you're here, angel. I missed you."

After dinner they went into the den and sat on the couch together, listening to soft music on the stereo. With her head resting on Hunter's shoulder, and his arm around her waist, Bliss experienced true contentment.

It was some time before she discovered that he was asleep. Slipping quietly out of his arms, she went to get her jacket.

Max came into the hall. "You're not leaving this early?"

"Hunter is exhausted. I didn't like to wake him, but he really should get into bed."

"Why don't you stay over?" Max asked casually. "I can put you in the room next to his."

"No thanks, Max." Her eyes brimmed with amusement at his transparent suggestion. "What Hunter needs is a good night's sleep."

As Bliss walked toward her apartment, Kirk was approaching from the opposite direction. She couldn't pretend not to see him, but her brief greeting was distant.

His confidence wasn't easily shaken, however. He gave her a big smile. "Hi there. I haven't seen you around lately."

"I've been away."

He eyed her golden tan. "Some fancy resort, I'll bet."

"Not exactly." She turned away. "If you'll excuse me."

"Do you happen to know where Shelley is?" he asked quickly. "I rang her bell, but she isn't home."

"I suppose she's at the studio. Why don't you go down there?"

He appeared undecided. "We might cross on the way. Maybe I'd better call and tell her to wait for me. Can I use your phone?"

Bliss didn't know how to refuse. There wasn't any reason to actually, except her dislike for the man.

He followed her inside. But after she had turned on the lights and pointed to the phone, Kirk was in no hurry to use it.

"This place sure looks different since that old bat moved out," he remarked, glancing around. "The room was so filled with junk you couldn't swing a cat around."

"Assuming one would want to," Bliss remarked derisively. "But you surprise me. I'd never suspect you wanted to swing with Mrs. Draper."

"Are you kidding? I was in here once to pick up the rent."

Which he no doubt pocketed. "You'd better call Shelley," she said, trying to hide her disgust.

"In a minute. I've been wanting to talk to you ever since the night we met. I'm afraid we got off on the wrong foot."

"It isn't important."

"It is to me," he murmured deeply. "I was attracted to you the minute I saw you."

"The same way you're attracted to Shelley?"

"I knew you got the wrong impression. She's good for laughs, but there's nothing heavy between us. Now *you're* somebody I could get really serious about."

"Any woman who would believe that has the IQ of a cantaloupe," Bliss stated crisply.

"Don't fight me, baby. We could make beautiful music together."

"Has anyone ever told you you're a walking cliché?" she asked disdainfully.

"No, but if you recite a few lines I'll fake it." He smirked, moving toward her.

"You're not even faintly amusing. Get out of my house, Kirk."

"You know that's not what you really want. I enjoy the chase as much as the next dude, but don't overdo it, doll face." He reached for her.

Bliss stepped back. "Don't be a fool. If Shelley ever found you here she'd throw you out like the garbage you are."

"What Shelley doesn't know won't hurt her."

Bliss gauged the distance to the door, but Kirk was blocking it. "If you don't leave this minute I'll tell her," she said, forcing herself to appear calm.

His low chuckle chilled her blood. "You don't think she'd believe you? By the time I got through with my side of the story, she'd be convinced you tried to rape me."

"Shelley isn't as gullible as you think," Bliss warned, backing away as he moved closer. "Everybody has a cutoff point."

"Let me worry about that. I have a feeling you're going to be worth it."

Bliss had retreated as far as possible. The wall cut off any further escape in that direction. As she started to move sideways, Kirk grabbed her.

"Let go of me," she commanded.

His eyes glittered with excitement. "Are you going to fight me? I like spirit in a woman."

"You're going to get more than you bargained for," she said through clenched teeth.

But when his arms closed around her, Bliss was defenseless. Kirk's morals were undoubtedly flabby, but his body was in top shape. She shivered with revulsion as his wet mouth closed over hers and his hands squeezed her breasts.

"Tell me you don't like this," he crowed triumphantly.

Without answering she struggled frantically, but that only incited him further. He rotated his groin against her, making her aware of his arousal. In spite of all her efforts, he dragged her toward the couch.

"This is it, baby. Playtime's over," he said hoarsely.

Bliss's arms were pinned back, and her strength was running out. She made a last effort to elude him when he pushed her down on the couch. Before he could pounce, she slid off the cushions onto the floor.

"Is that where you want it? Okay, anything that turns you on." He leered, falling heavily on top of her.

As he ripped her dress open, she sank her teeth in his hand.

Kirk reacted furiously. "You little hellcat! You'll pay for that." He was raising his other hand menacingly when the doorbell rang. "Who the hell is that?"

Bliss took advantage of his momentary distraction to squirm away and run to the door. Flinging it open she yelled, "Call the police!"

Nothing registered except the fact that help had come. As she tried to run outside, Shelley put a key in her hand.

"Go over to my place and wait for me," she ordered. "I'll clean up the mess on your floor."

Bliss was still trembling when Shelley joined her a surprisingly short time later. Remembering what Kirk had said about his power over Shelley, Bliss looked at her apprehensively. What she saw wasn't reassuring. The other woman's face was set in uncompromising lines.

"Are you all right?" she asked.

"I will be." Bliss moistened her dry lips. "It wasn't what you're thinking."

"You wouldn't want to know what I'm thinking," Shelley said grimly.

"He tried to attack me! Why can't you see that Kirk is no good?"

"I've always known that. I just wouldn't admit it to myself until tonight."

"You believe I wasn't responsible for what happened?" Bliss asked uncertainly.

"If you'd been interested in his kind of parlor games, you wouldn't have been trying to set a new record for the hundred-yard dash." Shelley poured Scotch into a glass and downed it in one gulp.

"I'm sorry," Bliss said in a muted voice.

"Don't be. You did me a favor." Shelley flopped down in a chair with her shapely legs stretched out. "I'm not stupid. I knew Kirk was a louse. Call it an obsession—or maybe great sex, I don't know. As long as he was making it with bimbos, I told myself it didn't mean anything. But when I saw him trying to rape you, I realized what a fool I've been."

"You saw us?"

Shelley smiled sardonically. "It's typical of Kirk that he didn't check to see the drapes were drawn. Maybe it's the actor in him. That's the one thing he does that deserves applause."

Shelley's flippancy didn't disguise her deep hurt. "I realize this is as traumatic for you as it was for me," Bliss said tentatively.

"Not really." Shelley raised her glass and squinted through it at the light. "After a period of mourning, which I expect to last about twenty minutes, I'm going to call David. The only acting he knows how to do is to act nice."

Bliss double-checked all her locks before she went to bed, although she was sure Kirk wouldn't return. She knew Shelley must have told him off in the four-letter words he understood. At least something good had come out of this horrendous night.

The stars were in all the right orbits from then on. Once Shelley had rid herself of Kirk's dominance, she allowed herself to appreciate David. They were like teenagers, stopping just short of holding hands.

Bliss's own life was just as rapturous. She and Hunter spent passion-filled nights together, although his days didn't allow him to be with her. Wrapping up the documentary took all his time. Max called Bliss almost every day, and sometimes she complained to him.

"Maybe I should go into show business. I got to see more of Hunter when we were working together."

"You don't want to get into that rat race. Look at it this way. You have quality time, that's better than quantity."

"You're older than you look, Max," she hooted derisively.

In spite of wanting to see more of Hunter, Bliss enjoyed the weeks that followed. She felt slightly guilty about not pursuing her teaching credentials more diligently, but money wasn't a problem and she hadn't had a real vacation in years. Her work on the documentary was finished, and she was free to do anything she wanted.

That palled eventually, about the time the movie was finally in the can. They had a gala wrap party on the set where everyone talked about future plans. Everyone except Bliss.

Her real reluctance to look for work was because of Hunter. The ideal time for them to get married would be while he was between projects. She knew he had another movie scheduled, but Hunter was being vague about it, so he could probably take some time off for a honeymoon.

Not that he'd actually proposed, but Bliss had a feeling he was waiting until he could give her his full attention.

At first Bliss didn't realize his phone calls had tapered off. She was out a lot and merely figured she'd missed him. Hunter didn't like to leave messages on a machine.

Then she began to see him less often. He broke dates or simply neglected to make them. When Bliss voiced her disappointment, Hunter professed to be equally regretful.

"It's always like this at the beginning of a production, honey, but things will settle down."

"Couldn't you have taken some time off before jumping into a new film?"

"I didn't want to give Dennison an excuse to put if off indefinitely. I've earned this one, and he's damn well going to deliver."

"Feeling the way you do about Clay, I'm surprised you're so gung ho about working for him again."

"I'm not, but he's the one with the checkbook. The script is what excites me."

"That used to be my role," she remarked in a small voice.

"Nobody can play the part any better," he said with a throaty chuckle.

"You must have a good memory."

"I do."

His husky tone encouraged her. "Will I see you tonight?"

"I wish I could, angel, but I'm having dinner with the new screenwriter I hired."

"I thought the script was already written."

"It is, but we've decided one of the major characters needs fleshing out. I'd tell you to wait up for me, but I have no idea how long this will take."

Bliss didn't care how late he'd be, but she wasn't going to beg. "Okay, if you'd rather talk shop than have the company of a compliant woman, that's your loss."

"Don't I know it! I'll try to get away tomorrow night."

He'd *try*! "I'm not sure about tomorrow," she said coolly. "I have a tentative date."

"That's good. I'm glad you're keeping busy," he answered, to her utter outrage. "I was beginning to feel guilty for neglecting you."

"I wouldn't want to distract you from your new movie," she said evenly.

"You're always a distraction, my love. I only— Hang on a second." He issued crisp instructions to someone in the office before coming back on the line. "I have to go, honey. My console is lit up like a cruise ship."

Bliss sat and stared at the phone, too dispirited to move. It rang a few moments later, restoring her faith. Hunter had realized she was upset!

"Hello," she said eagerly.

"What's new, kid?" Max asked.

"Oh. Hi, Max."

"I got a warmer greeting from the government when they drafted me," he commented.

"I'm sorry. I thought you were Hunter."

He chuckled indulgently. "Now I feel better. How's it going with you two lovebirds?"

"One of us is a homing pigeon and the other is a night owl. Not a great match, is it?"

"What's that supposed to mean?"

"I hardly ever see Hunter anymore."

"That can't be! He's out every—" Max stopped abruptly, then tried to cover up. "He's out of his mind to work so hard."

"Is that what he's doing?"

"The boss is like this every time he starts a new picture. He'll ease up as soon as things get rolling."

"If you say so," she answered tonelessly.

It was late that night when Hunter let himself into his darkened house. As he started for his bedroom, the lights came on and Max appeared in his pajamas.

"What are you doing up at this hour?" Hunter asked.

"I couldn't sleep. Did you and Bliss have a good time tonight?"

"I wasn't with her. I had dinner with Larry Hatfield, a writer I just hired."

Max stared pointedly at his cheek. "He has nice taste in lipstick."

Hunter scrubbed at his cheek in annoyance. "I ran into some actress I hardly knew. I think she puts her lipstick on with a butter knife."

Max watched his efforts stoically. "I talked to Bliss today. She said she hasn't seen much of you lately."

Hunter glanced through the mail he'd picked up from the hall table. "You know how it is at the start of production," he answered absently.

"That's what I told her. I *didn't* tell her you've been out every night."

"I've been working!" Hunter's temper was starting to rise. "Being a producer isn't a nine-to-five job."

"It isn't worth losing your girl over, either."

"Don't be ridiculous. Bliss understands this is just a temporary situation."

Max shook his head. "For a guy who's supposed to know so much about women, you're pretty dense."

"Stop trying to make trouble," Hunter ordered.

"You're already in a pile of it. Bliss won't wait around forever. Why don't you marry the girl and get it over with?"

"When I want your advice, I'll ask for it." Hunter stormed down the hall and slammed his door with a resounding bang.

"I hope it's not too late by then," Max muttered, staring after him.

Hunter phoned Bliss early the next morning. "I thought about you last night," he said softly. "Did you think about me?"

"Once or twice. I was watching *The Invisible Man* on television."

"I deserve that," he said ruefully. "Would you forgive me if I took you to Palm Springs for the weekend?"

"Do you really mean it?" she asked delightedly.

"You better believe it! I haven't seen you in so long I'm having withdrawal pains."

"I feel the same way," she murmured.

"It's all settled, then. The other thing I called about was a memo from the publicity department. They want to take a few more shots of you. Could you come to the studio this morning about eleven o'clock?"

"I'll be there. Maybe we could have lunch afterward," she said hopefully.

"Wouldn't you know I have a luncheon engagement?" He groaned. "But come to my office for a minute, anyway. I need to see your beautiful face."

Bliss left the house early so she could stop by his office before the photo session. If it ran late, she might miss him. But like many well-laid plans, hers didn't work.

"Mr. Lord is in a meeting with Mr. Dennison," his secretary informed her. "I'm afraid he won't be finished until lunchtime, and then he has an appointment."

"Yes, I'm aware of that. Do you happen to know where he's having lunch?" Bliss asked on an impulse.

"I made reservations at L'Etoile for one o'clock."

Bliss nodded, then went on to the photo studio. She was on good terms with all the publicity people, having dealt with them extensively. They had a fond reunion before getting down to work.

When it was over, Steve, the head of PR said, "You're a good sport to come in at such short notice."

"I think I deserve lunch, don't you?" she asked.

"You've got it. Where would you like to go?"

"How about L'Etoile?"

He whistled. "You have expensive tastes, but what the hell, it's on the expense account."

Bliss was hoping that Hunter would ask them to join him. He couldn't talk business *all* the time. When they got to the restaurant, she realized her concern was unfounded.

Hunter was sitting in a booth with a gorgeous brunette. Their heads were close together, and he was talking persuasively while she listened with a little smile.

Steve spotted them, too. "There's Hunter. We could say hello, but I don't think he'd appreciate being interrupted." He laughed.

Bliss had difficulty swallowing her lunch. Their table was in clear view of Hunter and his companion, but he never glanced away from her. Unfortunately, Bliss couldn't avoid looking at them. She'd seen that intense expression on his face before.

"For a woman who picked this place herself, you don't seem to be enjoying the food," Steve complained.

"I chose it for the ambience," she said brightly. "You never know who you're going to see here."

The phone was ringing when Bliss returned home that afternoon. She answered it listlessly.

"I'm sorry I missed you today, angel," Hunter said. "You wouldn't believe what this day was like."

"I think I have some idea."

"The good news is that I made a lot of progress."

"I was sure you would."

"Is something wrong? You sound funny."

Bliss had to admire the puzzled note in his voice. But of course he didn't know the deception was over.

"The least you could have done was be honest with me, Hunter," she said bitterly. "I can't say I would have been happy to find out we were through, but you should have told me to my face. Putting me off with excuses wasn't worthy of you."

"What are you saying? You must know how I feel about you."

"I do now. I was at L'Etoile today. I saw you with that woman."

"I *told* you I had a luncheon date. That was Marcella Lanzoni. I was trying to persuade her to star in *Winter's End.*"

"You have an answer for everything, but it won't work this time. I don't even know why you bother. A clean break is a lot less messy than dragging it out."

"Don't even say such a thing! I never realized you felt this way. Surely you know how much you mean to me."

"Why do you insist on pretending?" she asked hopelessly. "How can I believe you when we've drawn farther and farther apart?"

"If I didn't see that, then maybe *Winter's End* has become an obsession with me," he said slowly. "I've fought to make it for such a long time. But I'd chuck it in a minute before I'd risk losing you."

"I never wanted you to give up your work for me, Hunter. I only want to be part of your life."

"You *are* my life," he declared passionately.

"I wish I could believe that," she said uncertainly.

"I swear things will be different from now on. I'll make up for every lonely hour I've cost both of us. We'll make love all weekend the way we used to." His voice wove a sensuous spell as he described his intentions in vivid detail.

"It sounds like old times." She laughed breathlessly.

"It will be, my love."

"Can we leave early on Friday?" she asked eagerly.

"Well, I thought—" He hesitated for a moment, then his voice firmed. "We'll leave anytime you choose. God knows I owe it to you."

Bliss couldn't wait to tell Shelley the good news after crying on her shoulder for so long. The other woman had been wonderfully supportive through all her down periods, and they'd become good friends.

"You look like you just won the lottery," Shelley remarked when she answered the door.

"I did better than that. Hunter called. He's taking me to Palm Springs for the weekend."

"That *is* good news. It calls for a drink. I know, coffee for you. Come in the kitchen while I make it."

Bliss followed, giving an edited version of the things Hunter had said to her. "He was so shocked. If only I'd told him sooner how I felt."

Shelley listened fondly as Bliss told her again how wonderful Hunter was. Long before she'd exhausted the subject, the phone rang. Bliss could tell by the softened look on Shelley's face that it was David.

Not wanting to listen, she glanced at a tabloid-type newspaper on the kitchen table. It was a trade paper for people in the entertainment industry. Her gaze flicked with minor interest over glamorous couples at parties and restaurants. As she glanced down the page, Hunter's name leaped out at her. It was in a column called Wheeling & Dealing. Bliss's breathing almost stopped as she read:

Casting has begun on *Winter's End*, the made-for-TV movie Hunter Lord has been peddling unsuccessfully to all the networks. Rumor has it that Clay Dennison agreed to finance it as a bonus for getting Bliss Goodwin to sign on the dotted line. Even if *Winter's End* is a bomb, WBC got a good deal. Interest is running high on the only authorized version of the Goodwin story. Advertising spots are selling for premium prices, which spells big bucks for everybody.

Bliss was as rigid as a statue when Shelley returned.

"David sends his best." She took a second look at Bliss, then noticed what she was staring at. "Now don't go jumping to any conclusions."

"You knew about this all the time I was telling you how much Hunter loves me. How could you let me go on?"

"What does one thing have to do with the other?"

"He was *paid* to make love to me!"

"That's downright silly. You're not thinking straight."

"You're wrong. Everything is finally clear. Hunter had a special interest in keeping me happy. But after the documentary was finished, that was no longer necessary. Why waste time with me anymore when he'd already earned his bonus?" Bliss asked bleakly.

"If what you say was true, why would he ask you to go away for the weekend?"

Bliss's smile was a mere jerk of facial muscles. "Hunter has an inconvenient conscience for a con man. That weekend was supposed to be *my* payment. He even said he owed it to me, but I was too dumb to realize what he meant."

"Men don't make love to women out of guilt," Shelley stated tersely. "Whatever his motives were in the beginning, he's in love with you now."

"Which of us is the naive one this time?"

"What are you going to do?" Shelley asked anxiously as Bliss got up to leave.

"What I should have done weeks ago."

In her apartment, Bliss got a suitcase down from the top shelf and started to pack methodically, trying not to think about the shambles her life had become. She was no match for the people here. It was time to go back where she belonged.

When the phone rang she answered it automatically, although there wasn't one person in the world she wanted to talk to. Certainly not Max, who was so closely associated with Hunter.

"I can't talk to you now, Max. I'm packing," she said in clipped tones.

"Where are you going?"

"Back to Africa."

"You got to be kidding! Why? Does the boss know?"

"No, and you're not to tell him until tomorrow." Just in case Hunter had the decency to try to apologize. That was one ordeal she could avoid.

"I don't understand. What happened? If he did something, you should at least give him a chance to explain."

"Somebody already did it better than he could. Read the *Hollywood Chronicle*." She hung up the receiver, cutting him off.

Max didn't waste any time after reading the article. He telephoned Hunter at the studio insisting on talking to him when told he was in a meeting.

"This better be an emergency," Hunter said ominously when he came to the phone.

"I thought you might want to say goodbye to Bliss before she leaves for Africa."

"What kind of stupid game are you playing?" Hunter asked impatiently.

"She read an article about you in the *Hollywood Chron.* It sounds like you sold her down the river. Hunter Lord gets bonus for giving Bliss Goodwin the shaft."

"It wasn't like that at all! They would have torn her to bits. I protected her!"

"Don't tell me, tell her."

Bliss answered the door listlessly, wishing everyone would leave her alone. She turned pale when she saw Hunter.

"Were you really going to leave without telling me?" he asked quietly.

"It would have been easier. Go away, Hunter. I don't want to listen to any apologies."

"I have nothing to apologize for. Why didn't you ask me about that article in the paper?"

"Because you would have lied to me again."

"I've never lied to you." His face set in stern lines. "It's true that I was promised *Winter's End* in exchange for your name on a contract, but that wasn't a betrayal. I made a dignified documentary with your cooperation."

"You could have told me you stood to profit, too."

"You were so suspicious of everyone that you might not have signed. And then they would have made something you'd have hated."

"If that's true, why didn't you tell me later? After we became lovers?"

"Because you never seemed to trust me completely."

Bliss wavered, recalling her frequent doubts. Then her resolve hardened as she remembered how he'd cut her out of his life when she was no longer useful.

"You were always good at talking me around, although I don't know why you're bothering now. I'm letting you off the hook. You won't have to make any more excuses for not seeing me. You won't even have to give me one last weekend." Angry tears filled her eyes.

"You can't honestly think it was a final payment?"

"That was the most insulting part of all!"

Hunter reached in his pocket and brought out a small velvet box. "Nothing I say will convince you, but maybe this will. I picked it up today on my way to lunch with Marcella." He handed it to her.

"What's this?" She opened the box and found a beautiful pear-shaped diamond.

"It's an engagement ring. I was going to give it to you this weekend."

She stared at him incredulously. "You were going to ask me to marry you?"

He smiled for the first time. "I still am. Will you do me the honor of being my wife?"

"Oh, Hunter!" She felt like laughing and crying at the same time. "I don't know what to say."

"You can say yes, because I won't ever give you up."

"How can you still want me when I've been such an idiot?"

"I haven't been very bright myself lately. Will you forgive me?"

Bliss threw her arms around his neck, and for long moments his mouth devoured hers. Then he swept her up and carried her into the bedroom.

They undressed each other with frantic haste, murmuring passionate words of love. Hunter's caresses were fervent, moving erotically over her body until she arched her hips into his. The throbbing contact was so incendiary that he reached for her convulsively.

Their union was wild and sweet. Neither held anything back. When the storm reached its height they rode it out together.

Bliss remained curled in Hunter's arms afterward, resting her head above his heart.

"How did you know I was leaving?" she asked finally.

"Max told me. He also told me to marry you."

She smiled. "Dear Max. He always did say you wouldn't know what to do without him."

"Not true." Hunter's hand glided seductively along her body. "Some things I can handle very nicely on my own."

* * * * *

Silhouette Special Edition

COMING NEXT MONTH

#571 RELUCTANT MISTRESS—Brooke Hastings
The prophecy clearly stated that a tall blond *haole* would enter
Leilani's Hawaiian paradise, bringing both love and anguish. Was
irresistible Paul Lindstrom that man, and was their mutual destiny
one of passion or pain?

#572 POWDER RIVER REUNION—Myrna Temte
Their feuding fathers had snuffed out JoAnna and Linc's teenage
romance, but a Powder River High reunion relit the fuse. Could their
own stubborn wills stem an explosion this time?

#573 MISS LIZ'S PASSION—Sherryl Woods
Locking horns with angry parents was elementary for passionate
schoolteacher Elizabeth Gentry—until she confronted single father
Todd Lewis, who offered *her* some *very* adult education....

#574 STARGAZER—Jennifer Mikels
With a family scandal to live down, high-principled attorney David
Logan knew he should avoid kooky occultist Jillian Mulvane. But her
love potion proved extremely potent....

#575 THE LOVE EXPERT—Maggi Charles
Stacy Mackenzie suddenly found herself in uncomfortably close
quarters with sex psychologist James Ashley-Sinclair. Could she
possibly hold her own with this notorious love expert?

#576 'TIL THERE WAS YOU—Kathleen Eagle
Forest ranger Seth Cantrell had chosen quiet solitude. Skier Mariah
Crawford was always in the limelight. One night of passion changed
their two lives forever . . . by making them reckon with a third.

AVAILABLE THIS MONTH:

Silhouette Intimate Moments®

It's time . . . for Nora Roberts

There's no time like the present to have an experience that's out of this world. When Caleb Hornblower "drops in" on Liberty Stone there's nothing casual about the results!

This month, look for Silhouette Intimate Moments #313

TIME WAS

And there's something in the future for you, too! Coming next month, Jacob Hornblower is determined to stop his brother from making the mistake of his life—but his timing's off, and he encounters Sunny Stone instead. Can this mismatched couple learn to share their tomorrows? You won't want to miss Silhouette Intimate Moments #317

TIMES CHANGE

Hurry and get your copy . . . while there's still time!

INDULGE A LITTLE SWEEPSTAKES

OFFICIAL RULES

SWEEPSTAKES RULES AND REGULATIONS. NO PURCHASE NECESSARY.

1. NO PURCHASE NECESSARY. To enter complete the official entry form and return with the invoice in the envelope provided. Or you may enter by printing your name, complete address and your daytime phone number on a 3 x 5 piece of paper. Include with your entry the hand printed words "Indulge A Little Sweepstakes." Mail your entry to: Indulge A Little Sweepstakes, P.O. Box 1397, Buffalo, NY 14269-1397. No mechanically reproduced entries accepted. Not responsible for late, lost, misdirected mail, or printing errors.

2. Three winners, one per month (Sept. 30, 1989, October 31, 1989 and November 30, 1989), will be selected in random drawings. All entries received prior to the drawing date will be eligible for that month's prize. This sweepstakes is under the supervision of MARDEN-KANE, INC. an independent judging organization whose decisions are final and binding. Winners will be notified by telephone and may be required to execute an affidavit of eligibility and release which must be returned within 14 days, or an alternate winner will be selected.

3. Prizes: 1st Grand Prize (1) a trip for two to Disneyworld in Orlando, Florida. Trip includes round trip air transportation, hotel accommodations for seven days and six nights, plus up to $700 expense money (ARV $3,500). 2nd Grand Prize (1) a seven-night Chandris Caribbean Cruise for two includes transportation from nearest major airport, accommodations, meals plus up to $1,000 in expense money (ARV $4,300). 3rd Grand Prize (1) a ten-day Hawaiian holiday for two includes round trip air transportation for two, hotel accommodations, sightseeing, plus up to $1,200 in spending money (ARV $7,700). All trips subject to availability and must be taken as outlined on the entry form.

4. Sweepstakes open to residents of the U.S. and Canada 18 years or older except employees and the families of Torstar Corp., its affiliates, subsidiaries and Marden-Kane, Inc. and all other agencies and persons connected with conducting this sweepstakes. All Federal, State and local laws and regulations apply. Void wherever prohibited or restricted by law. Taxes, if any are the sole responsibility of the prize winners. Canadian winners will be required to answer a skill testing question. Winners consent to the use of their name, photograph and/or likeness for publicity purposes without additional compensation.

5. For a list of prize winners, send a stamped, self-addressed envelope to Indulge A Little Sweepstakes Winners, P.O. Box 701, Sayreville, NJ 08871.

© 1989 HARLEQUIN ENTERPRISES LTD.

DL-SWPS

INDULGE A LITTLE SWEEPSTAKES

OFFICIAL RULES

SWEEPSTAKES RULES AND REGULATIONS. NO PURCHASE NECESSARY.

1. NO PURCHASE NECESSARY. To enter complete the official entry form and return with the invoice in the envelope provided. Or you may enter by printing your name, complete address and your daytime phone number on a 3 x 5 piece of paper. Include with your entry the hand printed words "Indulge A Little Sweepstakes." Mail your entry to: Indulge A Little Sweepstakes, P.O. Box 1397, Buffalo, NY 14269-1397. No mechanically reproduced entries accepted. Not responsible for late, lost, misdirected mail, or printing errors.

2. Three winners, one per month (Sept. 30, 1989, October 31, 1989 and November 30, 1989), will be selected in random drawings. All entries received prior to the drawing date will be eligible for that month's prize. This sweepstakes is under the supervision of MARDEN-KANE, INC. an independent judging organization whose decisions are final and binding. Winners will be notified by telephone and may be required to execute an affidavit of eligibility and release which must be returned within 14 days, or an alternate winner will be selected.

3. Prizes: 1st Grand Prize (1) a trip for two to Disneyworld in Orlando, Florida. Trip includes round trip air transportation, hotel accommodations for seven days and six nights, plus up to $700 expense money (ARV $3,500). 2nd Grand Prize (1) a seven-night Chandris Caribbean Cruise for two includes transportation from nearest major airport, accommodations, meals plus up to $1,000 in expense money (ARV $4,300). 3rd Grand Prize (1) a ten-day Hawaiian holiday for two includes round trip air transportation for two, hotel accommodations, sightseeing, plus up to $1,200 in spending money (ARV $7,700). All trips subject to availability and must be taken as outlined on the entry form.

4. Sweepstakes open to residents of the U.S. and Canada 18 years or older except employees and the families of Torstar Corp., its affiliates, subsidiaries and Marden-Kane, Inc. and all other agencies and persons connected with conducting this sweepstakes. All Federal, State and local laws and regulations apply. Void wherever prohibited or restricted by law. Taxes, if any are the sole responsibility of the prize winners. Canadian winners will be required to answer a skill testing question. Winners consent to the use of their name, photograph and/or likeness for publicity purposes without additional compensation.

5. For a list of prize winners, send a stamped, self-addressed envelope to Indulge A Little Sweepstakes Winners, P.O. Box 701, Sayreville, NJ 08871.

© 1989 HARLEQUIN ENTERPRISES LTD.

DL-SWPS

INDULGE A LITTLE—WIN A LOT!

Summer of '89 Subscribers-Only Sweepstakes

OFFICIAL ENTRY FORM

This entry must be received by: Nov. 30, 1989
This month's winner will be notified by: Dec. 7, 1989
Trip must be taken between: Jan. 7, 1990–Jan. 7, 1991

YES, I want to win the 3-Island Hawaiian vacation for two! I understand the prize includes round-trip airfare, first-class hotels, and a daily allowance as revealed on the "Wallet" scratch-off card.

Name_____

Address_____

City_____ State/Prov. _____ Zip/Postal Code_____

Daytime phone number_____
                               Area code

Return entries with invoice in envelope provided. Each book in this shipment has two entry coupons — and the more coupons you enter, the better your chances of winning!

© 1989 HARLEQUIN ENTERPRISES LTD.

DINDL-3

INDULGE A LITTLE—WIN A LOT!

Summer of '89 Subscribers-Only Sweepstakes

OFFICIAL ENTRY FORM

This entry must be received by: Nov. 30, 1989
This month's winner will be notified by: Dec. 7, 1989
Trip must be taken between: Jan. 7, 1990–Jan. 7, 1991

YES, I want to win the 3-Island Hawaiian vacation for two! I understand the prize includes round-trip airfare, first-class hotels, and a daily allowance as revealed on the "Wallet" scratch-off card.

Name_____

Address_____

City_____ State/Prov. _____ Zip/Postal Code_____

Daytime phone number_____
                               Area code

Return entries with invoice in envelope provided. Each book in this shipment has two entry coupons — and the more coupons you enter, the better your chances of winning!

© 1989 HARLEQUIN ENTERPRISES LTD.

DINDL-3